JAKE LOGAN

SLOCUM AND THE RIVER CHASE

BERKLEY BOOKS, NEW YORK

SLOCUM AND THE RIVER CHASE

A Berkley Book / published by arrangement with
the author

PRINTING HISTORY
Berkley edition / March 1992

All rights reserved.
Copyright © 1992 by The Berkley Publishing Group.
Journal of the Gun Years excerpt copyright © 1992 by Richard Matheson.
This book may not be reproduced in whole or in part,
by mimeograph or any other means, without permission.
For information address: The Berkley Publishing Group,
200 Madison Avenue, New York, New York 10016.

ISBN: 0-425-13214-5

A BERKLEY BOOK ® TM 757,375
Berkley Books are published by The Berkley Publishing Group,
200 Madison Avenue, New York, New York 10016.
The name "BERKLEY" and the "B" logo
are trademarks belonging to Berkley Publishing Corporation.

PRINTED IN THE UNITED STATES OF AMERICA

10 9 8 7 6 5 4 3 2 1

HUNTED BY THE LAW—
AND THE OUTLAWED

Slocum watched a pair of hawks swooping far off over the trees. If they saw no evidence of the sharp-nosed man or the bounty hunter, they might get passage on a boat. Perhaps outrun them both. After all, it was not possible to watch every inch of the river . . .

He woke the general, and they looked to the cinches and prepared to go on. Mounting, they rode out to the road, and as they turned into it, the shots came.

General McRae fell from the horse. Slocum instantly threw himself off and lay in the grass, the Colt firing almost before he hit the ground. The shots came from brush on the far side of the road, and he fired at the source of the smoke, two, three, four, five times.

Suddenly it was quiet. Slocum crawled to McRae, who was huddled in the grass.

The general was hit!

SLOCUM AND THE RIVER CHASE

OTHER BOOKS BY JAKE LOGAN

RIDE, SLOCUM, RIDE
SLOCUM AND THE CLAIM JUMPERS
SLOCUM AND THE CHEROKEE
  MANHUNT
SIXGUNS AT SILVERADO
SLOCUM AND THE EL PASO BLOOD
  FEUD
SLOCUM AND THE BLOOD RAGE
SLOCUM AND THE CRACKER CREEK
  KILLERS
GUNFIGHTER'S GREED
SIXGUN LAW
SLOCUM AND THE ARIZONA
  KIDNAPPERS
SLOCUM AND THE HANGING TREE
SLOCUM AND THE ABILENE SWINDLE
BLOOD AT THE CROSSING
SLOCUM AND THE BUFFALO HUNTERS
SLOCUM AND THE PREACHER'S
  DAUGHTER
SLOCUM AND THE GUNFIGHTER'S
  RETURN
THE RAWHIDE BREED
GOLD FEVER
DEATH TRAP
SLOCUM AND THE CROOKED JUDGE
SLOCUM AND THE TONG WARRIORS
SLOCUM AND THE OUTLAW'S TRAIL
SLOW DEATH
SLOCUM AND THE PLAINS MASSACRE
SLOCUM AND THE IDAHO BREAKOUT

STALKER'S MOON
MEXICAN SILVER
SLOCUM'S DEBT
SLOCUM AND THE CATTLE WAR
COLORADO KILLERS
RIDE TO VENGEANCE
REVENGE OF THE GUNFIGHTER
TEXAS TRAIL DRIVE
THE WYOMING CATTLE WAR
VENGEANCE ROAD
SLOCUM AND THE TOWN TAMER
SLOCUM BUSTS OUT (Giant Novel)
A NOOSE FOR SLOCUM
NEVADA GUNMEN
THE HORSE THIEF WAR
SLOCUM AND THE PLAINS RAMPAGE
SLOCUM AND THE DEATH DEALER
DESOLATION POINT
SLOCUM AND THE APACHE RAIDERS
SLOCUM'S FORTUNE
SLOCUM AND THE DEADWOOD
  TREASURE
SLOCUM AND THE TRAIL OF DEATH
SLOCUM AND THE STAGECOACH
  BANDITS
SLOCUM AND THE HANGING PARTY
THE GRANDVILLE BANK HEIST
SLOCUM'S STANDOFF
SLOCUM AND THE DEATH COUNCIL
SLOCUM AND THE TIMBER KING
SLOCUM AND THE RAILROAD BARON

1

The carriage was black with red trim that was badly faded. It was a twelve-quarter coach, with all the panels in place because the night was chilly. The coachman, outside on the high seat, huddled in his greatcoat as the rig clattered along the cobbled street.

It had been raining, so the streets were wet and a low mist hugged the ground; a breath of wind off the bay hardly disturbed it. The coachman pulled his hat down and slapped the reins. This would be his last fare tonight. When he took this passenger to his destination he'd call it a day . . . It had been a long day. He could taste the hot toddy his wife would have ready . . .

It was near midnight, and there was very little traffic on the streets. It was the first cold night of autumn, after a warm summer, and San Franciscans were staying indoors, as sensible people should.

The coach approached the corner where gossip said the new opera house was to be built, and turned into Sentor Street, a narrow, dark little alley-like avenue that was gloomy even in daylight. But it was a shortcut— What was that? A whirlwind of shadows was suddenly in the street, and one grabbed the horse's bridle! A voice yelled at the driver to halt.

The driver hauled in on the reins in alarm. A robbery? What the hell!

One of the shadows threw open the coach door and held up a bull's-eye lantern, shining the light inside. The driver could see the man was masked.

The man said, "All right, come out of there, General."

"Who are you?" the passenger demanded.

The man with the lantern had a pistol. He cocked it, a menacing sound. "Out with you. Come on, hurry!" He pulled the passenger out, and another masked man grabbed him and hustled him into the dark.

The man with the lantern closed the tin, and it was suddenly gloomy. He growled to the driver, "All right, drive on. Go on . . ." He slammed the door and kicked the coach.

The driver slapped the reins, and the coach rumbled away as the driver looked back over his shoulder. They were mounting horses . . . then they were gone.

The kidnapping caused a sensation in the city. The man kidnapped was a very well known lawyer, Butler McRae, ex-Confederate general, friend of many in high places.

The coachman, Henry Poland, went directly to the police to report the crime. They questioned him: "How many of them were there?"

"I only saw three, sir."

"Would you recognize any if you saw them again?"

"No sir. They was masked."

"Masked! Damn. You said they called McRae 'General.' That means they knew who he was."

"Yes sir, that they did. I heard it clear. 'Come on out, General,' they said."

"Did they say anything else—call each other by name?"

The driver shook his head. " 'Drive on' is all. I seen they had some horses waiting."

"Ahhh. They had horses waiting."

"Yes sir. And I heard 'em go riding off when I drove away."

"Which way did they go?"

"I couldn't see, sir. It was dark . . ."

"And you're sure you wouldn't recognize any of them?"

Henry Poland drew himself up. "How should I! I don't traffic with the likes of them!"

" 'Course you don't. Sorry. All right. Did the general say anything to them?"

"He asked who they was, is all I heard."

"And they didn't tell him?"

"No sir."

"Where were you taking the general?"

"To his home. I picked 'im up at his office. It wasn't the first time."

"So you've driven him before."

"Oh yes, half a dozen times I guess, but never so late."

"And you got the impression the three men were waiting for you?"

"Yes sir, I did."

One of the coppers said to another, "They may have been watching the office and figured he was going home."

"Yes, and then hurried to get ahead of him . . ."

"Exactly. This was planned pretty good."

They let Henry go, and one of them even remembered to thank him.

Omaha was a prairie town between the Platte and the Missouri rivers. It was in fact on the Missouri, across from Council Bluffs. It was a town with a goodly German population, and John Slocum was there, visiting a woman friend, Gretchen Duhr. He had known Gretchen for several years; she was a widow, having lost her husband in the war. He had died in a forgotten skirmish at a dusty crossroads named Beaver Hill.

A comely woman, she had not remarried but had invested

their savings in a small saloon and was doing well.

She also had rooms to rent upstairs, and Slocum stayed in one. Gretchen had three rooms just down the hall, which was extremely convenient.

Meeting her was icing on the cake; he had just returned from a chancy fracas with some claim jumpers and was resting. In two or three weeks he would go and hit Fred Reardon for a job, but that was a long while away. For the moment it was pleasant sleeping late and looking forward to midnight suppers with her . . . then back to bed.

And then a messenger arrived.

The note was from Reardon: "Come to my office as soon as you can."

Reardon, a lawyer with an office in Omaha, handled cases and accounts for some of the most important people. He had contacts everywhere and a second office in San Francisco. Slocum had done work for him in the past and they were good friends. He saddled his horse and rode to the office that afternoon.

Reardon was a short man, wiry and energetic, seldom still. He wore a brown suit with brown boots and a mauve tie. He shook Slocum's hand and slapped his back. "Thanks for coming so quickly."

"Your message sounded urgent."

"It was—I mean it *is*. A man has been kidnapped, and he's got to be found."

Slocum thought of Gretchen and her warm bed. "But the Pinkertons can handle that, Fred. And there's a lot of them. I'm only one."

"I know about the Pinkertons. And yes, they probably could handle it. But I want *you* to handle it and I'll pay whatever you ask. Say yes, John."

Slocum smiled. Reardon was not a man to take no for an answer. "Is there a ransom note?"

"No. Not to date. Nothing's been received from them. The kidnapping was two days ago—in San Francisco."

"San Francisco!"

"Yes. The man kidnapped was General Butler McRae. It's been in all the papers."

"I haven't been reading the papers."

Reardon looked at him quizzically. "You're not thinking of getting married, are you?"

"No. Certainly not!"

"All right. How soon can you go to San Francisco?"

Slocum sighed. "I suppose I can catch the next stage . . ."

"We've got a train now, you know, the Union Pacific. You can be there in four days." He handed Slocum a card. On it was written: Lt. David Pike, SFPD. "He's in charge of the case and a good friend of mine." Reardon turned the card over. "This is McRae's office. The kidnappers may send a note there."

There was another address on the card, Reardon's San Francisco office. "What about a wife?"

"No wife. She died years ago. McRae is an honest and upright man. Since the war he's had one of the best law offices in California."

"You said he was a general."

"Well yes, he was a general in the Confederate army. When the war was over, he went west. He has a few relatives living there." Reardon tapped the card in Slocum's hand. "My partner in San Francisco is Giles Munch. I have already been on the wire to him, so he's expecting you."

"You were sure of me—"

"This is a challenge, John. When did you ever turn your back on a challenge? Giles will supply you with funds or anything else you need."

"You have no idea who may have taken McRae?"

"No."

"Did he have any enemies you know about?"

Reardon shrugged. "Not that I know about. I think the kidnappers want money. McRae is well known, heads a successful law firm—" He paused. "I got a letter from him a few weeks ago. He hinted about an event, a surprise . . . something out of the ordinary, anyway." He shrugged again.

"I suppose that could mean something—or nothing. Maybe he met a woman..."

Slocum sighed, thinking again of Gretchen. "Yes, maybe."

"Keep Giles informed as well, John. I'll wire Lieutenant Pike that you're working for me. That'll grease the skids with the police. Send me reports whenever there's anything to say."

"All right." Slocum went to the door.

"And watch your back," Reardon said.

2

San Francisco was a bustling city on a long neck of land, a peninsula that half enclosed the beautiful bay of the same name.

Slocum took a room in the El Dorado Hotel and went directly to McRae's office. His name was on the shingle—McRae, Reed and Howell—but a clerk told Slocum the general had been semiretired for five or six months.

"They say he's been working on his memoirs, sir."

"How many knew that?"

"All of us in the office, I guess... I don't know how many others. It's not a secret that I know of."

The clerk passed him in to Abner Reed's office, one of the partners. He was a man in his fifties, with a ruddy face and heavy figure. He was imposing in a black frock coat and silver-rimmed glasses. He was on his way to court, he said. He was very distressed because of the kidnapping. "It was a disgrace, such a thing happening in the city! This isn't some wretched hovel like Los Angeles. And to such a man like General McRae! A man everyone looked up to."

Slocum said, "I understand he was working on his memoirs."

"Yes, he said he was. I believe he had concluded a deal with an eastern publisher, though I doubt very much if the manuscript was finished."

"Did he work on it here in the office?"

"No, but he hasn't really taken part in the firm's activities for about six months. I believe the book took up all his time."

"Have you actually seen the manuscript?"

"That's a curious question. No, I haven't." Reed was surprised. "Do you doubt it exists?"

"No. But I'm wondering if that was the reason for the kidnapping."

"Ahhhh, that's interesting." Reed thought about it. "But he wouldn't carry it about with him . . ."

"No, but they might squeeze its whereabouts out of him."

"Damn! I hadn't thought of that!"

"Do you have his home address?"

"Yes." Reed wrote it out and passed it over. "Anything we can do to help . . . Please ask."

"Thank you."

When Slocum went out he noticed a man at the far end of the hall. He looked away when Slocum glanced at him. Slim and dark, wearing a loose suit that was very wrinkled. Slocum went down the stairs touching the revolver under his coat. Was he being followed? How would they know about him?

He dismissed the idea.

Were the kidnappers after the memoirs? Maybe McRae had written something in them—or someone *thought* he was writing something—that the person wanted concealed. It was possible . . . If they had intended to kill McRae they would have done it instead of abducting him, certainly. No, everything pointed to the manuscript.

He went directly to the police headquarters building and asked for Lieutenant Pike. A uniformed man escorted him upstairs and down a dusty hallway to a tiny office.

David Pike was a good-looking younger man, very straight

and tall, with blondish hair and a polite manner. Yes, he had received a wire from Fred Reardon—who had once saved his bacon. He owed Reardon, he said. He shook hands with Slocum and offered him one of the two chairs in the room. The office held a desk, the chairs, pegs on the wall for coats and hats, pictures and documents behind the desk, and nothing else.

As for the kidnapping, he had no clues at all, Pike said. "But I have informers everywhere. I'm hoping one of them will stumble over something that we can move on."

"What about the manuscript? That seems a good bet for a motive."

"Yes, I agree. But it hasn't turned up. It's not in McRae's office or his rooms." Pike spread his hands. "He did not have it with him the night he was taken. He had dinner with friends, and I've talked to all of them."

"Is it on its way to the publisher?"

"I'm told it isn't finished."

"Yes, Abner Reed said the same thing."

Pike said, "General McRae had connections to Confederate intelligence during the war. He must have known many secrets. I think you're right about the manuscript being the motive for the kidnapping. Someone wants it destroyed."

Slocum smiled. "Unless it's someone he helped put into prison."

"There's always that. But those threats are seldom carried out. And why would that kind of person kidnap him? Wouldn't he have shot McRae in the carriage?"

"Probably."

"I'll wire the publisher, just in case . . ."

"Good."

When he left Pike's office he took a hack and was driven to McRae's rooms; he lived in a suite at the Seaview Hotel. As far as Slocum could tell, he was not followed, but he knew that very experienced men would be almost impossible to detect.

The manager of the hotel was Ernst Hobble, a stout,

bearded man who greeted him gravely and looked at his credentials supplied by Reardon.

"You wish to look through the general's rooms, sir? You know the police have already done that."

"Yes. I've just come from them. I'm grabbing at straws," Slocum admitted, "but there may be something there . . . By all means send someone along with me."

Hobble sent a young clerk, and they walked up to the second floor, Suite A. As they reached the door the clerk was about to put the key in the lock when Slocum stopped him. "Wait . . ."

He put his ear to the door, hearing muted sounds from inside. Pulling the clerk away from the door he whispered, "Is there supposed to be anyone in residence?"

The clerk shook his head. "No, sir. The general lived alone."

"All right." Slocum drew his Navy Colt and cocked it. "Unlock the door and jump aside. We'll find out who's in there."

The young clerk nodded and put the key in the lock. He was very nervous and rattled the key against the metal—and suddenly a shot came smashing through the panel of the door!

Slocum kicked the door wide open and ducked low. He had a glimpse of a man behind a chair. The man fired, and the bullet whacked into the wall of the corridor as Slocum fired through the chair. The chair fell over; the man's boots appeared, and his pistol clattered away over the hardwood floor.

There were sounds from the next room, and Slocum crawled in and lay flat on the floor, the six-gun ready. How many were there? He was in a sitting room. To his left was the body of the man behind the fallen chair. There was a hole in his forehead. What the hell were they doing in the rooms—looking for the manuscript?

He moved forward slowly. A head appeared behind a cabinet, looking frightened. Slocum fired too fast; the head disappeared. Now he could see into the second room. They had torn the paneling off most of one wall.

A pair of feet came into view behind a desk across the room. Slocum aimed carefully and fired. There was a yell and the man fell heavily, smashing some glassware.

Slocum got up and eased into the room against the wall. Maybe there were only two of them. He looked around for the clerk. He was staring with round eyes, his cheeks pale as paper. Slocum said softly, "Get a doctor."

The lad nodded and ran.

The man across the room began to howl with pain. His foot was shattered. There was no more fight in him. Slocum picked up his gun and looked through the other rooms quickly, no one.

He gazed at the ruined paneling. So far they had found nothing. Had they intended to pull the paneling off all the walls? Thorough!

The wounded man knew nothing, he told the police with Lieutenant Pike. His name was Emilio, and he had been hired not to fight but to do carpentry. When someone had come to the door, the other had tossed a pistol to him and told him to help. He had not even fired it. And he had no idea what the other had been looking for.

What was the other's name?

All he knew was "Jack."

Pike had him put in the police hospital under guard.

He would attempt to find out the dead man's full name, Pike said as they looked through the rooms. There must be hundreds of men in the city named Jack.

The two intruders had looked into everything—linen closet, bath, bedroom; all the cabinet and dressing table drawers had been dumped on the floor. The entire suite was a mess. They had even taken knives to the bed mattress.

"But no manuscript," Pike said broodingly. "He *was* working on it. His partners say so."

"He hid it somewhere else, then."

"Why hide it? He didn't know he was going to be kidnapped."

Slocum nodded. "But maybe he received a threat. Isn't that possible?"

"Yes . . . that might be the answer." Pike smiled. "All right, where did he hide it?"

Mr. Hobble gave Slocum the name and address of McRae's housekeeper. She came in once a week, he said. Maybe she knew something.

But she did not. She lived nearby with an ailing husband. She had cleaned and ironed for the general for nearly a year, and he had been very kind to her and generous. But they had rarely talked. Usually while she cleaned the place he went for a walk.

A manuscript? Well, she had seen a stack of papers on his desk. What did a manuscript look like?

His relatives knew even less. They were distant cousins and lived across the bay. Pike had already talked to them. Slocum turned up nothing at all.

He came back on a ferryboat. It was dusk when the ferry pushed into its slip and discharged passengers and wagons.

The sniper fired a few seconds too soon.

He must have been nervous, or the light had been very poor, Slocum thought later. The rifle shot whacked into the side of a wagon an inch from Slocum's nose. He ducked under the heavy dray with the Navy in his hand. A second shot came from between two houses, splintering wood above his head.

People yelled and scattered, and the startled driver hauled back on his reins as Slocum raced across the street, drawing another shot that went wide.

He gained the side of the house, moved along it to the corner, and looked into the space between the houses. No one. He found a spot where someone had waited for a long while. There were numerous brown cigarette butts on the ground. Who wanted him dead? Probably the man who had paid the two to search the general's rooms. Someone wanted him to stop looking.

How many knew about the manuscript? A dozen... maybe more?

But how did the someone know about *him*?

There was no way Slocum could know how many the general had talked to about his manuscript. Who had the publisher talked to? It might be a very long list.

He decided to call on Giles Munch.

He took a hack to the office in the morning. Munch was a thickset man in his late fifties, dark and expansive. He was delighted to meet Slocum—"Fred Reardon has mentioned so many nice things about you." He had coffee and drinks brought as they sat in his very comfortable office looking out over the bay. He had known the general for many years. It was a damned disgrace, his kidnapping.

Slocum said, "Then you know about the manuscript?"

"I have heard about it. Never saw it, you know." Munch sipped coffee and peered over the rim at his guest. "I find myself doubting that it is a reality."

"You doubt it? Why?"

"I know that Butler was making notes for such a book, because he mentioned it to me, but I doubt he did much work on the project. If he had actually started to write it, I'm sure he would have said something to me about it. After all, we are old friends."

Slocum said, "No one else doubts it."

"Has anyone else seen it—or seen any part of it?" Munch smiled. "The publisher says he does not have it or any part of it. He bought the book only on Butler's name, you know."

"The police think the kidnappers took the general so they could force him to tell where they can find the manuscript."

"Hmm. Well, I think he was kidnapped for money. A ransom note will turn up. You'll see."

"I hope you're right."

3

Lieutenant Pike also wired the publisher, and Munch's statement was confirmed. The publisher did not have the manuscript. Maybe Munch was right—it didn't exist.

Slocum had come to a dead end. He went over the case with Pike, and they both agreed all loose ends had been tied up. There was no other place to look.

Unless someone was lying.

Was there a manuscript or was there not? If so, was it at the core of the case? Why had the general been kidnapped?

Slocum reported to Reardon, with a copy to Munch, that the situation was substantially unchanged. They were no closer to a solution than they had been a week ago. All leads had been exhausted. No ransom note had been received. The police were wondering if the general was alive.

Reardon replied: "Keep at it."

Then suddenly General McRae was found!

A bay fisherman on his way out to the fishing banks found him half drowned, clinging to a plank in the cold water, and hauled him aboard. Putting back to shore, the fisherman called a policeman, and the general was sent to a hospital.

It was well he had a sturdy constitution, or the general would surely have perished from exposure and exhaustion. When he was revived, the general told the doctors his name. Lieutenant Pike went to the hospital at once and on the way alerted Slocum.

McRae was wiry and gaunt, looking done in. But he was determined to tell them what he knew. "I was held on a boat," he said. "It was anchored several hundred yards out from shore. They kept me in a darkened cabin and shoved food through a small opening once a day."

Pike asked, "Did you see any of them?"

"Only when they first kidnapped me . . . and then they were masked. There were three of them."

Slocum asked, "Do you think you would recognize their voices if you heard them again?"

"Possibly. But none was especially distinct."

Pike asked, "Did they tell you want they wanted?"

"No. They said very little in my presence. Do this, do that, sit there . . . that sort of thing."

"What can you tell us about the boat?"

"Not much, I'm afraid. It was just a boat. When we approached the bay they put a blindfold on me and tied my hands. They led me to a rowboat and took the blindfold off only when I was in the cabin."

"Did they question you?"

"About what?"

Pike said, "About your memoirs."

"No. They did not. Why would they do that?"

"We suspect that was why you were kidnapped. Is there something in the memoirs that certain people would object to?"

The general sighed. "Yes, I expect so . . ."

"Then they do exist, the memoirs?"

McRae looked surprised. "Yes, certainly. I have worked on them more than a year."

"If they didn't question you," Slocum said, "it's possibly because they thought they had plenty of time. How did you get away?"

"A stroke of luck, I think. One of them came into the cabin every day—masked, of course—but the last time he was in a hurry and didn't lock the door properly. I managed to force it open and slip into the water. This was at night. The water was cold, and a strong tide took me away from the boat in a hurry—I'm not a good swimmer. The tide carried me toward the sea. The more I tried to reach shore, the more the tide pushed me away, or so it seemed. And when I thought I was about finished, the fishing boat appeared out of the mist and I called out . . ."

The doctor entered the room, frowning at the two. "That's all, gentlemen. He must rest. You may return tomorrow."

They rose and Slocum said, "Thank you, General. You're in good hands now."

Outside the room he asked Pike, "You're putting a guard on the room?"

"Yes indeed. There'll be a uniformed man at the door inside an hour. I'll have men investigate the waterfront, but I'm sure they've moved the boat by now."

"Yes, probably."

Lieutenant Pike returned to his office, and Slocum went back into the hospital. It was a small building, two stories high, with three doors—that he'd seen. Maybe there were more. It had not been built with an eye to security.

General McRae's room was on the second floor rear, a small room with a single bed, two chairs, and one window. It was Spartan and clean, with no pictures on the walls.

Slocum talked with the hospital director, a short, dark man with a pencil behind his ear. "I believe General McRae is in danger, sir. There will be a uniformed policeman on guard shortly, and I will come and go—"

"In danger—here?"

"Yes, I'm afraid so," Slocum said. "We must expect it."

"A policeman! I don't want to alarm the patients."

"The general's life is more important than some patients' worries."

The director sighed. "Very well . . ."

Slocum waited until the policeman arrived. He was Barry Knowles, a three-year veteran of the force, twenty-six years old, and powerful looking. Slocum showed him his post, outside the general's door; he would be relieved in four hours. No one was to go into the room without authorization.

That done, he went outside and looked over the building. If he wanted to get in secretly, how would he go about it? The easiest way would be to go in one of the doors, in disguise. But it would take more than one to kidnap the general again.

Maybe, if they decided the manuscript could not be found, their best course would be to kill the general so he could not duplicate it.

Slocum went back inside and into the general's room. McRae was asleep, and he stood looking at the man in the bed. There was no way Slocum could know what was in the kidnappers' minds, but he knew his own. He ought to get the general out and into another room.

He hurried back to the nurses' station. A middle-aged nurse was riffling through a stack of forms. She looked up at him as he paused before her. He said, "Is there another empty room on this floor, Miss?"

"Yes, there are two. Why do you ask?"

"I want to move General McRae."

She was surprised. "You want to move him?"

"For security's sake. The wrong people may know where he is now."

She stared at him, biting her lower lip. "I—I'll have to get permission . . ."

Slocum shook his head. "The fewer people know about this the better." He smiled. "Get permission tomorrow."

"You really think there's danger?"

"I know there is. Which is the nearest empty room?"

She rose, putting the forms aside. "I'll show you."

Knowles helped Slocum move McRae to a room across the hall. The general did not question them when Slocum said to him, "Security, sir."

The room they left was darkened, with the bed made up to look as if someone were in it. Knowles stayed inside the new room, sitting on a tipped-back chair, a revolver in his lap.

The nurses had a small kitchen downstairs. Slocum had a plate of food there with coffee, and he took a plate up to the policeman. Three hours had passed peacefully. A different nurse was on duty in the station. Slocum nodded to her as he prowled the hall restlessly.

Then suddenly a fusillade of shots erupted from the room the general had left. Slocum rushed to the door, drawing his pistol. He opened it, ducking low. Knowles came from the other room. "What is it?"

"Don't know yet . . ." Slocum crept into the dark room. The window was pushed up, and the curtains fluttered in a slight breeze. There was no one in the room. He ran to the window and looked out, and a shot slammed into the wall near him. There was a long ladder below the window. He held the Navy out and fired three times into the gloom at the foot of it.

When he looked out again, he could see no one. The intruders had gone.

The nurse lighted the lantern in the room, and they saw that the shots had shredded the bedding. Someone had leaned in the window and tried to kill the general.

Lieutenant Pike assigned another policeman, so there were two on duty during the day. He commended Slocum. "If you hadn't moved him, he'd be dead now."

The general had said the same thing.

Slocum asked, "Why are they trying to kill him?"

Pike scratched his chin. "Do you know where that damned manuscript is?"

"No, I don't. I'll ask him."

"Apparently no one else knows either. *Is* there a manuscript?"

"He told me he's worked on it for more than a year."

"Then it does exist."

"Yes. And he's hidden it somewhere."

Pike growled. "The kidnappers can't find it—and maybe don't believe there is one. So they want to kill him to prevent him from writing it. How do you like that theory?"

"I like it fine. It fits a lot of the facts. No one's tried to kill McRae for years but suddenly, when gossip circulates about a book of memoirs, someone gets edgy."

"McRae knows secrets and might tell them."

"Exactly." Slocum nodded. "We agree on the theory."

"Guarding him's not going to be easy."

"As soon as he can travel, I'll get him out of San Francisco. Can you put us on a train in secret?"

"I can give it a good try."

4

Several days passed and the general felt much improved. The doctors said he might travel by train, definitely not by stagecoach; the constant jostling would tire him out.

The tickets were bought, one-way to St. Louis, and baggage packed. The day was selected, and Slocum had a private session with the general.

"Is there anything special you wish to take with you, sir?"

"No, just ordinary luggage."

"What about your manuscript?"

"I thought you'd get to that." McRae smiled. "It is in a very safe and secret place, John. Don't worry your head about it."

"My only worry is that you've hidden it so well no one will ever find it."

"I'm afraid I don't follow you . . ."

"What if something happens to you? We'll all do our best to see it doesn't—but what if?"

"Hmmmm, I see what you mean. The person who has it doesn't know what it is. Suppose I write out its location and seal it in an envelope?"

Slocum nodded. "And suppose we give it to Lieutenant Pike to put in the police department safe—not to be opened until you say so—or until, pardon me, your untimely death?"

"Very well. That's agreeable. I'll write it out at once."

"By the way," Slocum said, "why did you hide it in the first place?"

"Because of threats that it must not be published."

"Had someone read any of it?"

McRae shook his head. "I showed it to no one." He sighed deeply. "But I *did* mention it and some of its contents to a few people . . . I know now I should not have."

"Yes. That's probably it." Slocum thought privately that someone concerned had heard of the memoirs who suspected that he himself, or someone dear to him, would be mentioned. Suspicion alone might push that person to stop the presses.

Slocum sent messages to both Reardon and Giles Munch saying he was about to move General McRae out of San Francisco.

Munch sent a return message saying he protested. The general would be better guarded in the city, he wrote. It would be far more dangerous traveling cross-country.

Reardon did not question the move.

Slocum replied to Munch, saying he would do all in his power to thwart any attempts on McRae's life. Secrecy was the ticket. He asked Munch to say nothing to anyone about the impending move.

Pike provided him with names, and Slocum spent half a day interviewing prospective bodyguards. He hired one, Henry Biggs, a promising young man who was familiar with Colonel Colt's product, and was agile and quick on his feet. Biggs was dark, with big hands and excellent eyes, and was not talkative. He tended to answer with yes or no, or a grunt. Slocum thought that might well be a plus on a long journey.

• • •

Lieutenant Pike flooded the depot with detectives and uniformed policemen. They questioned everyone they found, pretending to be looking for an escaped criminal. A number of suspicious characters were escorted away and told to stay away, and at midnight only a few people were in the waiting room with confirmed tickets for the eastbound train.

General McRae, well bundled up, was brought to the station in an ambulance, and four men carried him, on a stretcher, into the train compartment where Slocum and Henry Biggs were waiting.

The arrival was well timed, and in a few minutes the train pulled out, hissing steam.

It had all gone very smoothly. Pike's police had been very efficient. It worried Slocum that it had gone so smoothly. Then he told himself he was getting fussy. Their enemies had found no chance to get near. Enjoy the advantage while you can.

He stayed close to the general, with Biggs in the compartment next door. And as the cars rolled out of the city in the wake of the chuffing engine, his worries abated. They had seen no suspicious characters boarding the train. It was of course possible that their enemies would wire ahead and cause trouble some other place. It was not difficult to find toughs to do a piece of shady work for a price.

He and Henry Biggs kept a close watch at each of the scheduled stops, but no suspicious-looking persons came aboard. Had they finally left danger behind?

That question was answered at the water stop, Angel's Crossing. It was a tiny collection of shacks, a water tower, and maintenance sheds in the middle of nowhere. The padlocked sheds marched along the tracks with piles of material stacked between them. Looking out the window, Slocum saw no one around at all. He thought that odd. Usually the tower operator's family gawked at the train.

He and Biggs walked to the rear vestibule of the car, intending to keep a watch on the other cars.

But before they reached it, a sudden storm of bullets

erupted from the maintenance sheds closest to the car. Slocum swore and ran back to the general's compartment. The firing stopped a moment before he reached it and flung open the door. Jagged holes had been torn in the side of the car, but McRae was unhurt. He had rolled off the bed at the first shots and stretched out flat on the floor.

Biggs rushed to the shattered window, looking out. "Gone," he said, pointing.

Slocum followed the finger. Men on horses were disappearing into the trees. There was no possibility of their catching them.

They helped McRae back onto the bed. Slocum said, "That was quick thinking, General . . ."

"Something I learned in the war," McRae said with a wan smile. "Did you get a look at them?"

"I'm afraid not. It happened too fast. It looks to me like several men emptied rifles into the side of the car. And they knew just which compartment to hit."

"How in the world could they know that?"

Slocum shook his head.

In a few moments the conductor poked his head into the room. "Anybody hurt?"

"No—luckily."

"What the hell happened here?"

Slocum showed him the damage. "Some people tried to discourage us."

"That's never happened before!" The conductor's shoes gritted on broken glass. "Well, I'll have to move you, sir. Are you all right?"

McRae nodded. "I'm not hurt. Thanks."

"You're lucky."

The move was completed in short order. McRae was transferred to another compartment and, once the watering was finished, the train pulled out. Much later the conductor took Slocum aside to say the tower's operator and his family had been locked in one of the sheds. They had not been harmed.

"But one of my crew was outside on regular inspection while we was stopped. He noticed a cross had been drawn with chalk under the general's compartment window. It must've been put there in San Francisco. That's how they knew where to fire."

Slocum said, "Thanks." So someone had been very clever. And that someone had wired ahead and arranged the ambush.

Was he foolish to go on? Maybe Giles had been right—they could do a better job of guarding the general in San Francisco.

He discussed it with McRae, who wanted to go on.

There was no further incident on the train. McRae took his meals in the compartment. It was confining but safe. Five days later they reached St. Louis and went at once to the Clearview Hotel. Slocum watched, but it was impossible to tell if they were tailed from the train station.

The few days' rest had done wonders for him, McRae said. He was as good as new. He was eager to go out onto the streets for long walks, but Slocum vetoed it. He was positive their adversaries were preparing some new plan. The last one had been unsuccessful partly because of luck. The war was a very recent memory, and the general had acted without thinking; it had saved his life.

Slocum wired Reardon and Munch that they had arrived safely, but he said nothing about the failed attempt at the water stop.

Reardon replied, asking where they intended to go from St. Louis.

The general expressed a wish to go downriver to New Orleans, where he had lived for many years, and so it was decided. They would take a river steamboat, a most pleasant trip, McRae promised.

Slocum sent off the wires, then the three of them had dinner in the hotel dining room. McRae, feeling expansive, declared himself proud of the book he had just completed.

"It is filled with wartime episodes and stories concerning the famous—including General Lee himself."

"And secrets?" Slocum asked.

McRae smiled. "There are some surprises, I expect. Yes, some secrets. The Confederacy's most important secrets are well known to the federal government now, of course, but there are a few things . . ."

"I trust the manuscript is safe."

"It is in the keeping of a dear woman friend who lives outside San Francisco. She has been told the package is old family and business records. It is quite safe. She would never think of opening it."

Slocum said, "Your enemies may know all your friends, sir."

"Yes, very likely. But in this case they will not find her. She came to the city very recently using her maiden name. Her husband died in the war. To find her name they would have to go to the courthouse where she was married forty or more years ago. Sherman's army burned it down."

"Then it's safe," Slocum said, raising his glass.

Slocum made arrangements with the steward, and the three went aboard the *Olympia* at midnight. It backed into the stream immediately and started the long journey downriver.

McRae went to his stateroom at once, with two pistols. Slocum stayed on deck till they were well on the way. No one had boarded after them, and neither he nor Henry had noted anyone following them to the boat.

But if someone had, he could easily wire ahead to lay another ambush. They were not out of the woods by a long shot.

Slocum and Henry Biggs took the stateroom next to McRae's, and for the next several days all was peaceful. The two looked searchingly at every passenger on board and could detect no enemy. The most evil appearing person turned out to be a mortician going home for his daughter's wedding.

The steamboat stopped several times for wood and to take on or discharge passengers. At dusk it came into Kelly's Landing, nudging the heavy logs where tall iron baskets of burning logs lighted the scene. Sweating blacks heaved firewood aboard and stacked it near the fireboxes. Slocum and Biggs leaned on the rails above, watching everyone. The mate paid off the woodhawk and came back aboard; the bells clanged and the gangway was brought in.

But before the boat moved out, two men ran and jumped the several feet onto the main deck. Instantly Slocum and Biggs ran down to the deck and confronted them.

"Jump back," Slocum ordered. "You can't board this boat."

The two men, both rangy and tough looking, swore at him, and one drew a pistol, scowling at him.

Instantly Henry Biggs brought his pistol barrel down on the other's wrist. Slocum sent a fist into the second man's face. Both men howled in pain. The pistol dropped to the deck, and Slocum and Henry rushed the two to the side of the boat and heaved them into the water, splashing and yelling.

In a moment the boat had gone by, leaving them far behind. Biggs picked the man's revolver off the deck and shoved it into his belt. They had gained one shooter in the fracas. He grinned at Slocum.

But the mate came hurrying along the deck, obviously annoyed. "What if them two was payin' passengers?"

"Then you lost two fares," Slocum said. "We didn't like their looks."

"You goin' to tell us who we can haul and who we can't?"

"Simmer down," Slocum said softly. "Where d'you suppose those two were going?"

The mate rubbed a stubbled jaw. "Maybe to Natchez."

"Then we'll pay their fares to Natchez. That suit you?"

The mate nodded. "That'll do. See the steward."

5

General McRae was restless, hating to be cooped up in the stuffy little stateroom. "I'd rather take my chances than smother in that damned room."

Slocum relented. There seemed to be no enemies aboard. The general came out and mingled with the other passengers, taking his meals in the main salon, playing cards—but always with Slocum and Henry Biggs at his side, watching everyone who came near.

There were no further incidents.

At the next stop several families came on board—women, children, and farmerish-looking men carrying wicker baskets containing chickens.

When they reached the town of Hemming on the Missouri side, there was a great bustle. Passengers hurried off the boat with their baggage, many rushing to get on the stagecoach leaving for Springfield in the west. Others came clattering aboard with their valises and boxes. Crowds of laborers hauled baggage and cargo, stowing some below decks, but most was lashed on the main deck under the critical eye of the mate.

During this confusion Slocum insisted General McRae

remain in the stateroom with Henry Biggs. There seemed to be a delay in shoving off again. When Slocum went to see what was holding them up, he found men working on one of the boilers.

He was able to speak to the mate for a moment, and the other said, "It'll be an hour or two at the very least t'fix this here."

"And maybe more?"

The mate shrugged. "It could take all night—depends on our luck."

Slocum looked at the sky. It would be dark in an hour. He walked the deck in thought. A dozen or more strangers had boarded the boat, and no telling how many were enemies. He frowned at the town, where a few pale lights glimmered.

They didn't have to stay on the steamboat.

He went inside and entered the stateroom. McRae and Biggs had been cleaning pistols. They looked at him expectantly, and Slocum said, "When it gets full dark we'll leave the boat and go into the town. If we're lucky no one will see us."

Biggs nodded and McRae said, "You mean go overland?"

"Yes sir. We'll buy some horses. Are you up to it, General?"

McRae smiled. "In my time I've slept on the ground in the rain . . . with Yankees all around us."

The mate's two-hour guess stretched into five or six, and still men hammered and swore and the boat remained tied to the landing posts. Most everyone went to bed, and only a few lanterns were lighted in the main salon. It was after midnight when Slocum led the general out onto the deck with Henry close behind. A great many deck passengers were sprawled here and there in nooks and niches between piles of cargo, some snoring.

The men working on the boiler were on the river side.

Slocum led along the deck on the shore side to the gangplanks and across to the levee. They met no one.

Hurrying into the town, they found it mostly dark. There were no lights at all along the single main street. Even the saloons were closed.

But the livery stable door was open. Slocum struck a match and found a lantern. Lighting it, he moved to the rear and came to a room with an older man asleep on a cot. He shook the man awake.

"Sorry to get you up, but we need horses. Are you the owner here?"

"Yea..." The man looked at him blearily. "Is it mornin'?"

"No. It's about midnight." Slocum hung the lantern on a wire. The old man was redheaded and needed a shave. He rubbed his eyes and looked at each of them in turn. "The sheriff after ye?"

"Something like that," Slocum said. "Put your pants on."

The owner sat up and reached for a shirt. He pulled it over his head, threw off the blankets, and shoved his feet into jeans as Slocum went back to the street door. He saw no one and returned to the room. The old man stood up and winced, holding his back.

"The hosses is out back in the corral," he said. "Bring one o' them lanterns." He unhooked the one from the wire and went out into the night, holding it high.

Henry lighted one of the lanterns that waited on a ledge and followed them.

The owner leaned on the corral poles. A half dozen horses switched tails, looking at them in the mealy light.

"Take yore pick," the old man said.

Buford Stark folded the telegram and slid it into a pocket. The three were on a steamboat headed downstream. He didn't care much for that, because it made the job much harder. They could get off the boat at any point, on either side of the river.

He was a man in his early forties, a very well dressed citizen who had never been in a federal prison. He had served time in small jails, mostly when he was younger, a decade or more ago. He had small eyes in a pale face, a sharp nose, and a pointed chin. Women did not usually care much for him. They said he looked like trouble. And they were right. He dressed like a gambler. Most took him for a gambling man—which he was not. He was a man without a conscience.

He was being paid to eliminate General McRae. *Eliminate* was Stark's word. He liked the sound of it.

Unfortunately McRae had two competent bodyguards with him. Stark had sent two hardcases against them, and both men had been dumped in the river. One had broken bones in his wrist.

His information had been right concerning his opponents. He had been told that John Slocum was as dangerous a man as he would find anywhere. And so far that had proved to be the case.

They were on the steamboat *Olympia*. Stark had hired a small boat and had followed it and come across it tied to the bank at the little town of Hemming. The boat was undergoing repairs. Many of the passengers had left the wounded boat and were waiting for the next steamboat south.

Stark sought out the *Olympia*'s steward and asked for McRae. There had been no one of that name aboard. But when he described the general the steward nodded at once. Yes, he had been a passenger. But he had left the boat hours ago . . .

Where had they gone?

There were numerous possibilities. Stark went ashore and lighted a cigar to think about them. They could have gone back north—but wasn't that unlikely? A man like Slocum would not worry overmuch about the two men he had tossed into the river. He had headed south—he would keep going that way. Was he bound for New Orleans with the general? Or maybe Natchez on the hill . . . The general was known to be from one of the old Southern families.

They could also go west, or cross the river and go east.

But the best possibility, Stark thought, was to wait for the next boat and go south. He believed in his luck. He would pick up the trail somewhere ... He always had.

He walked into the town. It was early morning, and there was an eating house with a sign that said Open. He went in and had breakfast, sitting by the front window, away from the chattering crowd of boat passengers.

As he sipped the bitter coffee, his eye fell on the sign painted on a barn across the street: Livery.

Finishing breakfast, he went into the barn. An older redheaded man was raking out stalls. He looked up as Stark approached. "Howdy."

"Good morning," Stark said. "I'm trying to catch up to three friends. I wonder if you've seen them. They—"

"Three?" The old man nodded. "They was three strangers in here las' night. Woke me up, they did, wanting hosses."

"Ahhh. That must be them."

"I sold 'em hosses and fixin's. Said they was headed west."

"West?"

"Yea. They was goin' to Springfield."

"Hmm. Is there a river road?"

The older man nodded. " 'Course. But they—"

"I know. Let's look at your horses. I'll need a good mount and a saddle."

The river road was a road in name only. It was a trail, and sometimes not even that. It followed the river in a general way, often veering far inland, taking the course of least resistance, especially when it showed wagon tracks. It avoided swampy land and broken ground and occasionally lost itself in forested areas. There were no bridges, but luckily the water in all the creeks they met was low.

Progress south was slow. They rode several hours to

put distance between themselves and the steamboat. But when the trail became dim, they made camp and waited for dawn.

McRae asked, "Is there a chance, do you think, that we'll be pursued?"

"If someone is following us, we left a pretty broad trail, I'd say. The thing that worries me most is that they'll get ahead of us and set a trap."

"Let's hope they won't think of it."

"I've been wondering about them, the pursuers, I mean," Slocum said. "From the way we've been attacked, it almost seems that someone is hiring men to do a specific job."

Biggs looked at him, head on one side, and the general said, "I don't understand . . ."

"Well, for instance, when the railroad car was fired on, several men sent shots into the car, then rode off immediately, as if the job were done."

"They made no attempt to follow it up . . ."

"Yes. And the two men who came aboard the steamboat. They were hired toughs for certain."

"Yeah, true," Henry Biggs said, and they both looked at him in surprise. It was the most he had said for days.

McRae frowned. "Could it be that the system of our enemies will work in our favor in the long run?"

"Yes, I'm sure it will—if they keep it up. But we can't depend on that. They've had no success so far."

"So what do you think?"

Slocum shrugged slightly. "If it were me, I'd put the job in the hands of a good man and let him do it his own way, either himself or hire men to help."

McRae smiled. "I'm glad you're on our side."

"I have an idea—if you'll go along with it, General."

"What is it?"

"If we're right, that our pursuers are hired toughs, they may be provided with descriptions of us, but they have never actually seen any of us."

McRae smiled again. "The two in the river have."

"But I suspect they won't be bothering us anymore."

"What's your idea?"

"I wish you'd let your beard grow, General."

"Good idea," Biggs said, and the general nodded at him.

"If they're looking for a clean-shaven man, they might be fooled by that simple deception. Even a second's hesitation one day—"

"All right," McRae said. "My razor stays in its kit. I haven't worn a beard for ten years . . ."

In the morning they continued riding south. When they crossed a tiny creek where the ground was muddy, Slocum shook his head, looking back at the plain tracks. They were leaving a trail a three-year-old might follow, and no help for it.

Near midday they came to a settlement: a general store, two houses, some corrals and sheds, and a small barn. A road wended its lonely way west, and there was a landing of sorts at the riverbank.

Slocum halted them when he saw the roof lines in the distance. "I'll go take a look."

He slid off the horse and moved forward through the trees to a point where he could see the front of the store. A wagon waited there, with a gray mule in the shafts. There were no horses on the street. Two older men sat in tilted-back chairs in front of the store in the sun. He saw no one else.

He went back to the others and they approached the store, looking about. The two citizens stared at them as Slocum got down and nodded. "Howdy. Any strangers in town?"

"Jest you-all," one of the men said. "You lost, are ye?"

"We're following the road. What d'you call this place?"

"Orkney's. This here's Orkney's store. You got any news?"

"No. Haven't heard any."

Thomas Orkney was a man in his fifties, lean and hollow-cheeked. He was sitting half asleep in a chair by the big black stove in the center of the room, his feet up on the ring. He woke when they entered, as the bell over the door rang fussily. He yawned and got up, stretching.

"Mornin' folks. You bring any news?"

"I hear they're fighting in Europe," the general said.

Orkney stared at him and moved behind the counter. "Who the hell cares what they does in Europe? Y'all folks looking to lay in some vittles?"

"I reckon," Slocum said. "How far's the next town?"

"Benton? Oh she's maybe half a day."

"Big place?"

"Oh yea." Orkney nodded. "Must be five, six hunnerd there. Not countin' mules."

They bought bread and canned goods, some tobacco, and a small bottle of brandy. The general said he liked a nip at bedtime. Orkney put it all in a gunnysack, and Biggs tied the sack on behind his cantle.

They rode several miles along the trail before stopping to eat. It made him nervous, Slocum said, to stay in the settlement. Too many nooks and crannies to shoot from.

They halted in a draw and picketed the horses between them and the trail, where they could watch the horses' ears.

But they were not disturbed.

Orkney's guess was good. They reached Benton just before dark. It had a single street, at right angles to the river. There was a ferry and a well-traveled road that wandered off to the northwest. They put up at the only hotel, which had seven tiny rooms, and the clerk told them they were maybe a hundred miles, give or take a dozen, from the Arkansas border. No one had measured it by the road; it was an agreed-upon estimate.

He also asked them to remove their boots before getting into bed.

6

Buford Stark had no trouble following the tracks of the three men along the river road. They were apparently the only travelers along it for days, in either direction, and the hoofprints were sharp and clear for the most part. He wondered if they knew they were followed.

When he came to Orkney's store he bought airtights and cheese and discussed the weather with Orkney, mentioning that he'd seen no one along the road.

The old man said, "You's the fourth one to come along in a week. They was three here just yesterday."

"Is that right!" Stark said in mock surprise.

"Said they might cross the river. They's a ferry at Benton."

"Yes. They could be heading for Memphis."

"They didn't say. I got fresh ground coffee, you want some."

He stayed only an hour in the little settlement, then continued south along the river trail. Had they crossed the river? The fact that they'd mentioned it to Orkney made him think they might. By mentioning it they wanted anyone following to think they had not. He smiled to the trees around him. That was a game he could play endlessly.

When he approached Benton, he circled the town and looked it over from a short distance, seeing no horses in the street. He rode in from the south and got down in front of one of the two saloons. There was no one else in the room, and the bartender was playing solitaire on the bar.

"Not many travelers," Stark said, sipping a beer.

"They comes in bunches mostly. Ain't had but a few this week. Guess it depends on the weather."

"Is the ferry still running?"

"Sure. Twict a day, regular." The barman looked at a turnip watch. "Next one in about two hours."

"I'm meeting my uncle here..." Stark described the general. "Wonder if you've seen him?"

"Was he with a couple others?"

"Yes. Two others."

"Then I seen him yesterday. Maybe he's at the hotel."

But the hotel clerk said he had left.

"Did he say where he was going?"

The clerk shook his head. "Guess he got mixed up in his times..."

"He's forgetful," Stark said.

At the landing he asked the ferryman, "Did three men go across with you this morning?"

The man squinted his eyes at the far bank. "Les'see, they was two boys and a woman with some geese—"

"Three men traveling together."

"Nope. Not this morning."

"Thanks."

Stark climbed on the horse and headed south again. Maybe they didn't know they were followed.

He had only a very loose plan in mind, and he was prepared to take advantage of circumstances or chance. His orders were to get rid of the general—no one cared how he did it. He much preferred to ambush the three—maybe he could hire some help in that. But there was no hurry about it. In fact, the longer the general thought he was safe, the better it would be for Stark. Surprise was always the best weapon in the world.

Slocum led the way out of Benton. The trail was only a single-track path, and the brush closed in on both sides; the trees met overhead and it was gloomy, but the ground was hard. After a mile he halted and got down, walking back, looking at their tracks.

"What is it?" McRae asked.

Slocum returned and took off his hat, ruffling his dark hair. "We have to expect we're being followed. And this looks like a good spot to begin evasive measures." He grinned. "If we're not, there's nothing lost."

"What do you propose? Hiding our tracks?"

"More than that. I suggest we circle around and go back to Benton through the woods. Then we can take the ferry across the river, and if we're lucky we can lose whoever it is."

McRae nodded. "All right. Let's do it." He glanced at Henry, who smiled.

Biggs led them off the trail, and Slocum went back and carefully brushed out every vestige of their passing. Satisfied, he mounted again, and they moved through the woods into the town and down to the ferry landing.

The ferryman had made one trip, and the next was not on his schedule for four hours. "You'll have to wait, gents," he said.

"When you go, how much for the three of us?" McRae asked.

"Fifty cents apiece, with the hosses."

The general reached into his pocket. "I'll give you five dollars for a crossing right now." He handed the man a gold piece.

The ferryman took it, looked at McRae—and smiled.

Buford Stark followed the river trail all that day and toward dusk came to Havers, another tiny settlement hard by the river. It seemed to be a fisherman's town. There was a cove of sorts, curving in from the river, where a dozen or more boats were tied up. Onshore a few small boats were pulled out of the water, and one was being painted.

He asked for beer in the deadfall and described the general to the barkeep, saying the man was his uncle. "He came through here, probably yesterday."

The other shook his head. "Not through here, he didn't."

"There were two men with him."

"No. We don't git us all that many strangers. You're the first for two days. T'other'n came from south on a mule. Most of our trade comes from the river."

Everyone he talked to said the same thing. The three men had definitely not come to this burg.

Stark thought it over. Maybe they had turned off . . . Or had Slocum outsmarted him? He could have backtracked or taken another route. Stark swore. He'd lost an entire day. There was nothing to do but go back to Benton and start over.

There was no hotel and no livery in the settlement. He camped in the woods and slept fitfully. In the morning he ate out of a can and chewed bread as he rode back north, feeling grumpy.

In Benton, Stark discovered the three had gone across the river. And that told him something else: They knew they were being followed.

It occurred to him, now *he* would have to be on the watch for an ambush.

On the Tennessee side the land was more open, but there was no river road. When people traveled in this part of the country, they apparently used the river.

The three he followed were at least a day's ride ahead of him, from the condition of the tracks last time he'd seen them. He looked longingly at the small boats gliding by on the great river, carried along by the current. He hurried south, watching for tracks . . . and found some. Then lost them again where the ground was hard. Finally he found them again, and they led him to the town of Warren.

It was in a valley alongside a stream that swirled into the river. The town had a telegraph, a hotel, and even a small playhouse.

But did it also shelter the three men?

When they arrived in Warren, the general looked very tired. He declared himself fit, but Slocum could see the signs, and he decided they would stay over and rest in the hotel for a day or two.

It was a two-story building and advertised nine rooms: fifty cents per night, stable feed extra. It also had a barbershop next door, and there was a restaurant across the street. At the river, the end of the street, was a planked landing with a string of lanterns that were lighted at night for steamboat roustabouts. There was a steam ferry that chugged across the river and back several times a day like a fussy old man going to market.

The town was the center of a farming community, and nearly all the steamers that stopped took on produce for sale up or down the river; they seldom discharged or took on passengers.

Slocum was certain they were followed—but by whom? It was annoying as hell not to know. So the only sensible thing was to keep the general locked in his room, to admit no one without the secret knock. Of course McRae hated it, but it could mean death from a sniper if he showed himself. Slocum even asked him to stay away from the room's windows.

Henry Biggs brought the general all the newspapers he could find, but he had no idea how to play chess, which the general loved. Henry had never seen the game before. He remained in the room with two pistols handy, while Slocum acquainted himself with the hotel's other guests and looked at each newcomer narrowly. But there were very few of these. The hotel usually did a feast-or-famine business, one of the clerks told him, very busy at times and mostly empty others.

The hotel had twelve rooms, but the owner lived in one, and two others were rented for the year by older people who had sold their farms.

It was an edgy time for Slocum, not knowing who was after them. He wired Reardon and Munch, telling them where they were and that the general was in good health. He did not mention future plans.

But he worried about staying in the hotel for any length of time, because it was probably the first place an enemy would look for them. McRae was reasonably safe in the room, with Henry there with him; between them they had four guns.

He itched to move on.

He thought about going on board a steamboat . . . except that it was much like a hotel, confining. To go aboard they would have to show themselves, and he doubted they could disguise each other enough to fool a watcher. They might only look foolish and attract more attention.

It would be much easier to slip away from the hotel in the dead of night. With the aid of a little cash, he was certain he could arrange with the stableman to agree to help.

He discussed this plan with the general, who declared himself rested and fit—and eager to get out of the room.

Slocum then had a talk with the stable owner, a wiry old-timer who had lost a leg at Malvern Hill and now hopped about with a crutch. One of their party, Slocum said, had married a girl in Kansas City and had taken her to his home in Charleston. But now her brother had decided an ex-rebel was not good enough for her, and he had sworn to kill the new husband.

The stableman, who had fought for Bob Lee, was disgusted to hear this sad news and quickly agreed to do whatever he could. Slocum wanted him to take their horses out of town and picket them somewhere in secret. The stableman said there was an old barn, unused at the moment, that would do admirably. It was outside the town a mile or so, and he drew a rough map and described the barn. He would take a bunch of horses down that road in the evening, he said, and leave their three in the barn. Unless someone was incredibly watchful and actually counted the horses, he would never suspect. Slocum gave him one of the general's gold pieces.

The stableman also had a suggestion. There was a road leading south; it was two or three miles to the east, used by a few farmers; it would lead them to the town of Landros.

"A stranger won't know about it. You cut east from the barn and they's no way you could miss it."

Slocum promised him the bride would be grateful.

With McRae following and Henry Biggs bringing up the rear, they left the hotel by the privy door near midnight. The town was silent and dark. They walked by alleyways to the road the stableman mentioned, and down it to the barn. There was a lantern just inside the door, the man had said. Slocum lighted it, and they saddled the horses and were on their way in minutes.

7

Buford Stark came into Warren, dusty and hungry. He went at once to the hotel with his story of meeting an uncle. He described the general and was surprised to hear that such a man had not stayed there.

"He was with two others."

"There were three men," the clerk said, "but one of them was bearded."

Stark snapped his fingers. "I forgot to mention that. Are they still here?"

The clerk shrugged. "I'm afraid your uncle left last night."

"He left at night? Was there a steamboat at the landing?"

"Well, we're not sure. He left payment in his room, so he could have gone at any time. There are steamboats coming and going, you know."

Stark thanked him and went out. So the general had grown a beard. Well, that wouldn't help him. He went along the street to the livery. It was run by an older man with one leg. Stark described the general, with beard, saying he was an uncle. "He was with two others."

The stableman seemed suddenly hostile. "I ain't seen 'em."

"Of course you have! Their horses were here in your stable."

"They's plenty of other places in town to keep hosses."

Stark pushed the older man into a stall. "Where did they go?"

"Goddammit! You got no right to—"

Stark drew his Army .44. "Where did they go?"

"They didn't tell me!"

"So they *were* here."

"They was here, but they didn't tell me nothing." He pushed at the other. "Lemme out, dammit!" His voice rose shrilly.

Stark brought the barrel of the revolver down on the man's forehead and shoved him violently. The crutch clattered away, and the man fell back into the straw, eyes staring, and didn't move.

Stark leaned down, frowning. He hadn't meant to hit that hard . . . But he had. The man was dead. There was no pulse.

Swearing, Stark put the pistol away and looked around. It was dim back in the stable; no one had seen them. He went to the wide front door and looked out into the street. No one was near. He went back, dragged the body to the rear, and piled it on a cot, covering it with a blanket. Then he remembered the crutch and went back for it.

What a damned nuisance. He hadn't gotten the information he'd come for. And now it was best to get the hell out of town. The hotel clerk would tell the law about him, for sure.

He mounted his horse and rode east slowly, turning south when he reached the end of the town street. Passing the last of the tents, he drew the Colt and looked at the barrel. A slight smear of blood. He grabbed some leaves from a tree and wiped it. What a nuisance.

He looked for tracks and found none. Had they gone aboard a steamboat? If so, they were a hundred miles away by now. What was his best course? Probably to keep going south. When he reached a town with a telegraph he'd wire and maybe learn something.

He continued to look for tracks, moving from the river to a mile or so inland, and found nothing.

They had probably taken a steamboat.

The road the stableman told them about was mostly a two-track trail where wagons had been rolling for a long time. It was joined by another coming from the distant hills, and it took them at last to Landros, a town the size of Warren, but it was dying.

The town was on the bight of a river loop, but the river, in one of its temperamental changes, had curled away from the town and was now a mile away, where a new settlement was growing up along its bank. The telegraph line was still in Landros, and Slocum sent off two messages giving their progress, mentioning his fears.

They put up at the hotel, a ramshackle building rapidly going to seed. The rooms were barely better than stalls in a stable. The only restaurant in town served tough beef and bitter coffee, and they were glad to leave the place behind after a night's restless sleep.

There was no road at all leading south, but there was a road of sorts, they were told, on the Arkansas side. They took a flatboat across, big enough to take the horses.

Slocum was much relieved when the boat pushed into the muddy bank and they clambered off. Possibly they had left a pursuer behind. But the worry that an enemy would get ahead of them and set an ambush ate at him.

How many were coming after them? Too many unknowns.

The general was also showing signs of fatigue again. He was much older than they, and Slocum was concerned. The constant riding and sleeping out under the stars was taking its toll, though McRae never once complained.

They desperately needed a place to hole up for a while.

Stark reached Landros in the middle of the night and slept in the stable beside his horse until dawn. After breakfast in a steamy restaurant, he sent a wire and in several hours received an answer. McRae and his companion had been in Landros only a day before. Only one companion was mentioned. Apparently Slocum had hired a helper on his own.

And they had not taken a steamboat. Stark had been warned that Slocum was as wily as they came. Possibly Slocum hoped *he* would take a steamer and go hunting hundreds of miles downstream fruitlessly.

He quickly learned, too, that the three men had crossed the river again. They were probably very close. It was time for him to hire his own helper: someone who had spent considerable time on the shady side of the law and who had no great fear of consequences—or conscience.

He spent a busy time in one of the several deadfalls in Landros and selected one man out of half a dozen who were interested in easy money, and who owned rifles. The man, Jim Bird, was dark and lean, admitted to a year or two in jail, and had supported himself of late by accosting pilgrims in lonely places. In a time when every man drank, Jim Bird drank too much. But he did not tell Stark that.

Stark agreed to pay him in gold and gave him twenty dollars in advance. Bird agreed to do whatever was required of him, knowing it was a job of shooting.

He had a horse, and he and Stark crossed the river late in the afternoon.

They found the river road at once, only a stone's throw from the bank, but there had been considerable traffic along it, and he could detect no particular tracks that might have been made by the three he pursued. But he headed south.

In the first little river burg they came to, Stark found pay dirt. Yes, he was told, three men of that description had been through but did not stop long, only a short time ago.

Maybe five or six hours. The older man was bearded.

Stark was jubilant; he was closing in. But it was getting dark. He and Jim had to make camp before dusk. Their prey might turn off the road, and they would miss them in the dark if they went on. Stark fumed, but the wait was necessary.

"You aiming to shoot all three of 'em?" Bird asked.

"Not unless we have to. One is all I want, the bearded one. He's the oldest."

"What you want him for?"

Stark shrugged. "I don't care anything about him one way or the other. It's just a job." He smiled. "Same as it is to you."

Jim Bird nodded. He could understand that. Just a job.

The river made several huge loops, and they followed one around, not knowing the lay of the land at all, and thereby lost a day's travel. Slocum led them across the next loop, saving untold miles. They lost the road also but picked it up again on the third loop, where deep-rutted wagon tracks made it evident.

They slept out three nights, and finally smoke on the horizon led them to Barco. It was a larger town than the last, being a center of roads. It had another ferry and a steamboat landing, which was a half mile from the town square.

When they reached the town and got down in front of the hotel, Slocum saw how McRae half fell out of the saddle and hung on to the horn for a long moment, his face gray with fatigue.

He took the older man's arm. "You all right, sir?"

McRae smiled wearily. "Just a little tired. I'll be glad of a bed."

"How about some hot food first?"

"I'd like a bit of soup . . . then I'll have a sip of brandy."

Henry put their horses in the hotel stable, and they signed for two rooms. In the restaurant the general had soup, then ate half a steak with his dollop of brandy.

The hotel rooms were small as prison cells, but McRae fell into his bed and slept the clock round—to wake considerably refreshed . . . and hungry. His new beard itched, too, he said. It was growing in dark with patches of gray and made him look like a saloon hanger-on, he thought. It would likely be another week before it could be properly trimmed.

They had supper in the restaurant. Barco was a farming and traveler's town, taking its name from the oldest inhabitant, long departed. They ate steak with small round potatoes, grown just outside of town, the waiter told them. He recommended the apple pie, baked by the owner's wife.

Over coffee Slocum said, "I think we ought to go on tonight. Are you up to it, sir?"

"I feel excellent," McRae said. "The few hours' rest was all I needed."

"Good. Then we'll go later."

After supper they rested again, and toward midnight Slocum got the general up while Henry went down and saddled the horses. Earlier they had bought canned goods, and Henry divided them and tied the sacks on carefully.

The next town was called Ferris, according to the clerk, and was quite a way farther south.

They rode out slowly, taking the alley to the river, then moving south along the dimly seen road. There was a chill wind blowing off the water, and the moon was a slim crescent, ice colored and distant. The road wended its careless way through a scattering of trees, and the only sound was the rattling of dry leaves above their heads.

The first shots came as they rode into the clear, out from under the overhanging trees. Slocum felt the tug as a slug hit his saddle horn and *spang*ed off into the night sky.

He turned instantly, yelling to McRae to gallop back toward the town. He pulled his revolver and sent four shots in the direction of the sniper's muzzle flashes. Henry Biggs was firing, and Slocum saw Henry slap the rump of the general's horse and get between him and the ambushers.

McRae pulled up and fired back as Slocum shouted at him again to go on. But McRae emptied his pistol before obeying.

Two men were firing at them from a clump of trees. Slocum stood in his stirrups and aimed carefully, holding the Colt in both hands. He squeezed off two shots, then turned. He galloped after the general and Henry—and suddenly Henry's horse stumbled and went down heavily. It kicked as Henry jumped clear, then was still.

Slocum reined in. "Get up behind me." It was obvious the horse was dead.

Biggs shook his head. He uncinched the saddle and pulled it off. "Want this."

Slocum looked back as he reloaded. No more shots were coming from the trees. It was very dark, and apparently they were far enough away so they could not be seen. Henry tossed the saddle up onto Slocum's horse, behind the cantle, and Slocum saw the dark stain on Henry's coat.

"Are you hit?"

"A scratch is all."

The general came back to them. "Get up behind me, Henry." He helped pull the other up, and they rode back into the town.

Slocum was troubled. Maybe that lost day had done it . . . they had been spotted and the ambush set up for them. How much of it was luck? Because they had never seen their pursuers, one or more of them had been able to get close enough to watch them or to guess their movements. It was like fighting ghosts.

The hotel clerk was asleep behind the desk; they woke him and he directed them to the town doctor, who lived on a side street. They found his shingle and rapped on the door till he shuffled down the hall and opened the door, putting on his glasses.

He looked at them and stood aside. "Come in, come in— which one of you is hurt?"

Slocum said, "Take off the coat, Henry." He helped pull it off. Henry's arm was bloody and he gritted his teeth.

"In here," the doctor said. He led them into a side room that smelled of medicine. Lighting a lantern, he pointed to another and Slocum struck a match. The room was a medical office. On a desk there was a neat sign: Rufus Johnson, MD.

The doctor patted a high bench. "Sit here, please."

Henry slid up onto it, and Johnson cut away the shirt and washed the wound quickly. "It didn't touch the bone. You're lucky, young man. An inch to one side..." He whistled. "You might have lost the arm."

A woman came into the room, fully dressed. She nodded to them and the doctor said, "Let's put a dressing on this, Irene."

Slocum and McRae went into the hall and sat on the chairs lined up there. McRae said, "He took one intended for me."

"Yes, I'm afraid so. He put himself between you and them. He'll do to ride to hell and back with."

McRae scratched his beard. "If only he didn't jabber so much."

Slocum laughed. Not bad, for a general.

His shirt and coat were ruined, but Henry was well bandaged. It hurt some, he told them, but not enough to cry about.

"It was a clean wound," the doctor said. "It'll start itching pretty soon, which means it's getting better. In a short time you'll forget about it. Come and see me if anything changes." To Slocum he said, "Do you know who shot him?"

"No. A holdup man, we think."

Johnson shook his head sadly, and the general handed him a five-dollar gold piece. "Thank you, Doctor."

The doctor's wife brought an old coat and hung it on Henry's bare shoulders. "Wear this till you get something better."

"Thank you, ma'am."

They went back to the hotel for the rest of the night. They had fired a lot of shots at the clump of trees. Had they hit anyone . . . whittled down the opposition?

For the first time Slocum wondered whether he should have left the general in San Francisco after all.

8

Stark and Jim Bird rode into Barco after dark. Like hundreds of other transients, they were inconspicuous. No one paid them any attention. Stark related his usual "uncle" story to a hotel clerk and learned that the three men were indeed registered. He asked the clerk to say nothing to the three—he wanted to surprise them later; the clerk agreed.

Stark and Jim Bird sat in chairs across the street the next morning and watched Slocum go in and out several times, once bringing a gunnysack into the hotel.

"Two bits says they're moving out tonight," he said to Bird.

"You figger they think they've lost us?"

"I'd bet on it. Let's keep a watch. You go round and find a spot to watch the stable. I'll stay here. If they go, they'll head south and we can get ahead of them."

Jim nodded and left.

He saw Slocum in the hotel doorway toward dark; the other was looking at the sky. He was obviously fit and capable, a damned dangerous man who would not scare easily. But a bullet would go through him like any other.

It was a long wait, but when the three men came down to the stable hours after dark and began to saddle the horses, Jim Bird came hurrying back to Stark. They mounted and rode out to the river road, looking for a likely spot.

They found it in a clump of trees, just beyond a wide clearing. Even in the dark, Stark said, they ought to be able to do the job. "It's the bearded one we want."

"How can we tell that in the goddam dark?"

"Then we'll have to hit all three," Stark said.

This time the wait was short.

But when the three men came along the road, walking the horses, Jim Bird nervously fired a moment too soon. He aimed at the lead horse, but in the poor light he missed, and the three turned back at once, firing as they went. A fusillade of shots pounded the clump of trees. Stark emptied his revolver and buried his head until the shooting stopped. Three men could fire a hell of a lot of lead!

When he got to his feet, the three had gone, swallowed up by the gloom. Stark said softly, "Le'ssee if we hit anything . . ."

He walked toward the road, then turned. "Jim . . . ?"

There was no answer. He went back to the trees. Jim Bird lay facedown in the weeds. Stark turned him over. There was a black hole in his neck, and he was as dead as he would ever be.

Stark cursed a blue streak. He was on his own again.

He sat down on the grass, feeling that Lady Luck had kicked his butt. Of course any gunplay was dangerous, and no one could be certain he'd come out of a fracas alive . . . but this kind of luck was more than he needed.

He got up and dragged the body deeper into the woods, to where their horses were tied. He found the twenty dollars he'd given Jim and a few more in Jim's pockets, ignored Jim's horse, and rode back to town, making a circle to come into it from another direction.

He could not go to the hotel, not after the story he'd given the clerk. When the body was discovered, or if any of the three had been hit, the law would be looking for him. If someone happened to ask the clerk, he'd remember the "nephew." But the description he'd give would fit any of a hundred men. Stark needn't worry his head about that.

He went into a livery and slept in a stall beside his horse. In the morning he sent off a wire but did not mention the shooting. He reported only that he was closing in on the general.

The general gave Henry money and directed him to buy shirts and a coat at the local dry goods store. Henry's wound was reddening the next day, seemed to be bleeding slightly, and was hot to the touch. Late in the day it was definitely swelling, had a faint odor, and was discoloring.

Slocum insisted they go at once to see the doctor. Johnson removed the bandage, sniffed, and said, "Infected."

He cleaned the wound carefully, saying it took very little to cause an infection, but no real harm had been done. He bandaged the wound again, and they returned to the hotel.

Henry bore it all stoically, gritting his teeth. He had slept poorly, but that night he slept the night through, and in the morning he reported that most of the swelling had gone down. He was on the road to recovery.

Slocum replied that in that case they would go on.

However, that day there was a stir in the town. Someone had found a saddled, riderless horse a few miles along the river road, and a quick search and the smell of the dead had led them to a body in the woods. The deceased had been a man about thirty-five, poor as a frog and shot in the neck. No one recognized him, and the deputy decided he had been the victim of an armed robber.

The body would be buried in the local boot hill at county expense; the county had taken possession of the horse and saddle to be sold at auction.

Slocum said to the general, "We hit one of 'em, sir."

"Yes, it seems that way. Was there nothing on the body to tell who he was?"

"Apparently not."

"Poor soul . . ."

Slocum looked at the other in surprise. "He was a bushwhacker! He tried to kill us!"

"Yes." McRae sighed. "When do you want to go on?"

"A few hours after dark."

They took the river road again, this time without incident. It was well marked by wagon ruts for about ten miles, then the road forked. One branch led away from the river, and the wagon ruts went with it.

After the fork the road became a trail, half hidden by weeds. It was a byway probably used, Slocum thought, by no more than five persons since the world began. The country was sparsely settled at best, and very few found it necessary to go this way.

The next town, Ferris, was a long way off. They halted at sunup and made breakfast over a small fire, and McRae examined their back trail with binoculars for many minutes but saw no one.

Henry Biggs's arm was much better, he declared. "Don't hurt much." The ugly color had disappeared, and it did not feel hot to the touch.

They had ridden half the night and decided to sleep for several hours. Slocum took the first watch and walked to a point where he could see the river. Far out on its shifting-colored waters a few small boats were gliding downstream, and he wondered if their enemies were on one of them.

They had been going south determinably; an enemy might easily decide they would continue that way and take a boat to get ahead of them to lay an ambush. He had worried about that before; it was a very real worry.

Of course the most obvious way around the problem was to go some other direction. He studied the broad river, thinking. Why not go west? They could leave the river behind, perhaps make a large circle to come back to it farther down—if they so desired. They might lose the pursuers entirely.

Of course a trip cross-country, staying off roads, would be hard on the general. But it would keep him alive. And that was his purpose.

He discussed the idea with the others, after all had had a few hours' sleep. Henry merely nodded agreement. The general thought about it a few moments.

"You think there's danger of an ambush?"

"Yes, certainly."

He sighed deeply. "Then we'll go west as you suggest."

They had to make their own trail. It was easy going at first. The land was broad and flat for the most part, with forested areas and meadows. Slocum picked the paths of least resistance. They were not concerned with time or an objective. The weather was good, and they could take all summer if they wished. Maybe the longer the better. Their enemies might get disgusted and give it up.

They stayed well clear of the distant farms they saw and met no one. Slocum sought out hard patches of ground and led them over each one; if a tracker followed them, that might hold him up... a short while. They traversed pine forests where, from the look of it, no one had ever been before. The recent war had not touched this part of the land.

In deference to the general, Slocum set a leisurely pace that would not tire him out. They made each camp early while there was plenty of light, and did not set out at dawn, as he would have preferred. With the general's binocs he kept a close watch on their back trail and was certain they were not followed.

They were away from the river nine days and came back toward it cautiously, slowly, and when they saw evidences of a town on the horizon, Slocum went into it after dark to look it over.

It was called Norton Springs and had a small military post nearby. It was also on the river and had a landing and a telegraph line. He wired Reardon and Munch that night, saying they were safe and the general in good health.

The town had two hotels, and they put up at one of them, quickly heating water for the metal tub in the washhouse. They each soaked in the tub, then had supper in a restaurant, feeling like aliens recently returned to earth.

It was not torture, eating beans out of cans for nine days, but if that time went on much longer, it would qualify.

9

Buford Stark lost his quarry. The three men had suddenly disappeared, and he could not figure how. He went as far as Ferris but could discover no one in the town who had seen them. A group of older men sitting in chairs along the street swore to him that three men such as he described had definitely not come into town.

He had to conclude that they had not come this far. They had turned off somewhere and he had missed it.

One of the hotel clerks showed him a map of the region and spread it out on the desk. Stark pored over it. The map was hand drawn and showed the river, roads, and towns with distances penciled in. But the clerk said they were only guesses. Also the river had changed course a bit since the map had been made. The river was continually changing course, and no one would ever stop that. A river as powerful as the Mississippi would do as it damn well pleased, and humans had to accept it or leave the area.

The map did not help him much. If the three had left the river road they might have gone in any direction. It was possible that the fight, where Jim Bird had been killed, had changed all their plans. Had they gone back upriver? Everything was guesswork.

But he had one ace to play. The telegraph.

In Ferris he sent off a wire and in two hours received a reply. The three men had not reported in for a week or more. "Stay in Ferris," the wire said, and he moved into the small Riverfront Hotel.

Days passed before he received the wire that read: "They are in Norton Springs."

He left immediately.

The general shaved off his beard. He had been seen with it, and the reason for it had gone glimmering. He was glad to get rid of it, he said. It was more trouble and took more time to keep trimmed than to shave every day.

Henry Biggs's arm was nearly healed, and he had almost full use of it again. He had only a twinge from it now and then, he told Slocum.

Things had changed for the better. Slocum felt he could slightly relax his eternal vigilance—and then suddenly found out he could not!

As they left the hotel by the front door to go across the street to the restaurant for supper, Slocum caught a glimpse of a figure on the roof of the opposite building. Instantly he shoved the general aside, and a shot went between them and shattered a chair.

McRae fell, sprawling full length on the boardwalk as Slocum fired three times at the shadowy figure, then ran across the street and into the restaurant. He sprinted through it with the pistol in his hand, ignoring startled patrons and waiters, into the kitchen, pushing surprised cooks out of his path. He slammed through the rear door and ran to the alley, to catch sight of a horseman far down the lane, who quickly disappeared into the gloom.

He stared after the sniper, reloading the Colt and swearing. How had he known they were in the town? Was someone reading his telegrams to Reardon and Munch? Both men had staffs; but presumably no one but the man in charge was supposed to read the wires.

He went back into the restaurant, apologizing to those he had pushed, and in the dining room the town marshal stopped him.

"What was that all about?"

Slocum explained that someone had fired at him and his friends from the roof of the building. "He climbed down and rode off before I could reach the alley."

"You know who he was?"

"No."

The older man cocked his head. "Does that make a hell of a lot of sense? You don't know who was shootin' at you?"

They walked outside, and the general and Henry came across the street. "He was shooting at me, Marshal."

The marshal turned and his eyes widened. "You're General McRae!"

McRae nodded. "Yes—did we serve together?"

"Damn right! I was with your boys at Petersburg. You won't remember me but I seen you often along them damn trenches. I was a sergeant in Belmonti's Brigade."

McRae put out his hand. "I'm glad to meet you again. What's your name?"

"Tom Hendricks, sir. The boys won't believe it when I tell 'em . . ." He paused. "A sniper shot at you and you don't know why?"

"We're not sure, Marshal. Will you have supper with us? We were about to sit down."

"I'd like to, General, but I've got people to meet on my rounds." He nodded to them and touched his hat. "I'll see you-all again." He left, crossing the street.

Inside, they selected a table. Slocum said, "I expect that's not unusual, meeting someone you served with?"

"Not at all unusual. I've even met some in San Francisco." He smiled. "There were a lot of us, you know. Not enough, of course, and too poor to win, but we did what we could."

"You sure as hell did!"

The fall, when Slocum had pushed the general out of the way, had shaken him up more than he at first realized. He was bruised and very stiff the next morning and stayed in bed an extra hour. He was past the time, he said ruefully to Slocum, when he could wrestle on the grass and never notice it. Now he had to pay for such things.

Marshal Hendricks came to visit him at the hotel, and the two sat for hours talking about the war. And Hendricks offered his farm as a place to stay for a few days. It would not be known to the sniper, and they could relax for a time. There was no one there but a foreman and a work gang who had a bunkhouse. No one was living in the main house; his wife had died several years past.

Slocum urged the general to take the offer, and he finally did.

When they left, to make it more difficult for an observer, Hendricks and his three deputies scoured the area and flushed out several men who were camping along the road. When they were gone, Slocum led McRae and Biggs down to the stable where they met Hendricks, who escorted them to the house, five miles outside the town.

It was a small house, a mite dusty because it had not been lived in for a spell, but it would do nicely as a hideout. Hendricks talked to the foreman and returned to town.

Stark quickly located the general and his two companions. They were staying in the Kregar Hotel, across from a two-story building that had a restaurant on the ground floor and living quarters above.

He investigated and found a back stairway that went up to the rooms on the second floor. From there it would be an easy climb to the roof. It seemed made for a sniper. He could leave his horse tied below by the stables and get away down the alley. He made the climb to the roof and walked across it to the street side, where there was a chest-high parapet. He looked down into the street, estimating the distance to the hotel door was perhaps sixty feet.

All he had to do was wait until the general came out the hotel door. One well-placed shot should do the trick. Then down to the horse. He'd be a half mile away before anyone realized where the shot had come from.

But the plan had certain drawbacks. He could not stay on the roof all afternoon. Someone was sure to wonder about the horse, and the roof was directly across from the second-story hotel windows. Unless he sat down behind the parapet he'd be in plain sight.

However, the three he pursued would likely go to the restaurant for supper, it was so convenient, so his wait on the roof might not be long. If he remained motionless he might not be noticed by anyone glancing out of a window for that short time. It was a chance he had to take.

And it paid off. Almost.

When Stark saw the three come through the hotel door, he swung the Sharps rifle over the parapet and took quick aim. But Slocum caught the movement and shoved the general aside as the shot missed cleanly.

That sonofabitch Slocum! Stark swore as he ducked. Slocum's shots slammed into the parapet and went whistling into the dark sky. He ran across the roof, climbed down to the stairs, and took them three at a time to the ground. He piled on the horse and dug in his spurs. Did the man have eyes in the back of his damned head? He leaned down, fearing shots as the horse raced along the alleyway, but none came. He glanced back, half expecting to see Slocum on a horse, but no one followed him.

He had failed to hit the general.

However, he could be sure that Slocum had not gotten a good look at him. He had probably been only a shadow on the roof at that hour, and anyhow Slocum's glance had been very brief.

When he came back into town the next day, the clerk

told him the three had left the hotel. Stark had figured they would go into hiding after the sniping attempt; the clerk had no idea where they'd gone. He stopped at the other hotel; they were not there either.

He paid out money to hangers-on along the waterfront and could be sure, from what they told him, that three men of their description had not taken a steamboat, or any boat for that matter. The three had not come near the landing.

They might have holed up in one of the houses in town, and if so, he'd probably not find them, but was it likely? How would they know anyone in a town they had just come to?

It was possible they had taken one of the several roads leading out of town, but not the one following the river south. He had camped along that one and watched it particularly. Maybe they had camped in the woods nearby and had not left the area.

He had played hunches before. Now he decided to wait and see if they showed themselves. It seemed to be his only chance.

And while he waited he would enlist another helper. He talked to half a dozen and settled on one man who had a similar background to the late Jim Bird. His name was Charlie Bannon—he said. Stark had an idea it was not his real one, but he did not press it.

Charlie had spent a few years on a work gang and admitted to other stays in local jails. He had no real compunctions about gunning down someone—if there was a clear escape route open, and he was well paid. He was lean and dark, with a drooping mustache, and seemed shifty. He owned a Sharps and a horse and not much else. Bird had looked more trustworthy, but Stark figured to keep an eye on him. He did not tell Charlie what had happened to Jim Bird.

The general hated to admit he was not as fit and agile and able to take sharp knocks as he once had been, but it was apparent to Slocum that he was glad to arrive at the little house.

They went inside and lighted lanterns. Biggs put the horses in the stable, and McRae went to bed at once.

In the morning Slocum rode around the farm to get an idea of the layout. It was ideally located on level land, with plowed areas and orchards that were well cared for. He saw men working in the fields; the foreman waved to him. The man had been told they were in the house.

While Henry was in the stable rubbing down the horses, Slocum talked to McRae. "This place can't be defended. Our only defense is secrecy, and if any of that work gang mentions in town that we're here, we may be in real danger."

"Then let's not stay."

"I agree. Do you feel rested enough? I think we could remain here another day."

"I'd appreciate another day . . ."

"All right. Then that's it."

But by the second day McRae was restless. There was nothing at all to do in the little house, and Slocum insisted he stay inside. He was delighted when Slocum said, "We'll leave in the morning. Henry, you go into town to buy grub. Meet us later on the road south."

Henry raised an eyebrow and Slocum said, "You go in because they may not recognize you—whoever they are. The sniper must have gotten a good look at the general and me."

McRae said, "You don't feel there's danger in his going into town alone?"

Slocum smiled. "It's you they want, General. Not him or me. If they recognize him as one of us, the worst they'll do, I figure, is follow him to us."

Henry nodded. He saddled his horse and took the road into town.

Slocum and McRae went across the fields toward the river. By early afternoon they were on the river road, waiting in a grove of trees for Henry.

10

Buford Stark did not recognize Henry Biggs, who was only one of many in the town, as one of the three men he pursued. But when he saw a rider with a full gunnysack of eatables tied on behind the cantle, taking the road south out of town, he motioned to Charlie and followed.

It was not unusual for a rider to be packing food in such a fashion, but this one was the only horseman heading south with such a sack in the several days he had been watching.

"He's meeting the others," Stark said. "Bet you a gun."

His hunch was working.

He and Charlie followed a long way back, out of sight of the rider, tailing by means of the fresh hoofprints on the soft ground. They had to move slowly, not knowing what was ahead. Stark had no wish to walk into a trap. They followed for perhaps five miles.

Then, in spite of his care and watchfulness, Stark was dismayed to see the rider's tracks turn off the road and head into a grove of trees.

He hissed at Charlie to keep moving. "Don't look at those trees! We're just two travelers along the road."

"But sure'n hell they in them woods," Charlie said.

"Yeah—but maybe they've gone on—they're three to our two. Don't look, damn it!"

"What you gon' do?"

"Ride on past. Like I said, they're three to our two. We have to catch 'em when they're not looking. That one, Slocum, is a sonofabitch."

"Maybe they'll go back into town."

"Not when they just bought a sack of grub. I bet you they'll go across the river again. Slocum is tricky as hell."

"Which one is Slocum?"

"He's the big one. They say he's dangerous as a rattler." Stark looked at the sky. It would not be dark for hours. If they went back now and were seen, Slocum would know for sure they weren't ordinary travelers. But the chance had to be taken. They were too close. He motioned and turned, heading north, moving off the road toward the river.

When Henry Biggs joined them in the grove, he said he had not spotted anyone following him. "I kept lookin' back."

But the two men had followed.

With the general's binoculars, Slocum examined the two riders from the shelter of the brush and trees. As they came along the road they were obviously interested in the tracks, and he saw that both followed them with their eyes, off the road and into the trees. Then they jerked their eyes away and went on past. Now he had no doubts. One of them was the sniper.

One man, better dressed than the other, had small, squinty eyes, a sharp nose, and a pointed chin. He had to be the one who was after the general. The other was an obvious tough, rough appearing and probably a jailbird, with the brains of a sidewinder.

Slocum did not hesitate. "Let's go toward the river. Maybe we can get across."

McRae had watched him. "You figure those two were the ones?"

"Yes, I think so. Henry, lead the way."

Slocum brought up the rear. The two after them would probably circle around as soon as they were out of eyesight and try to come up from a different angle. Slocum slipped out his Navy and examined the caps. They'd give the two a hot reception.

It took a half hour to arrive at the riverbank. They could see no boats at all in either direction. Slocum pointed north. "Let's ease back that way..."

They had to go slowly, wending their way through thick copses of trees and heavy brush. Several miles along the bank they came on a flatboat. Four men were poling it upstream in slack water, moving at a snail's pace.

Slocum hailed them, asking them to come inshore. They poled the boat into the muddy bank and one, who seemed to be the leader, put his hand to his ear.

The general urged his horse as close to the water as he could and offered the man a five-dollar gold piece. "Take us across?"

The man looked around at the others, who nodded at once. Five dollars, gold, was a week's wages.

They quickly put out planks, and the horses were walked across and tied securely. The four were going back to Cairo, where their families were. They eked out a living carrying cargo to ports downriver and poling back. Poling a boat was damned hard work; they were saving money to buy a small steamer, so the gold piece was very welcome.

The flattie was light, unloaded, and bobbed across, landing far downstream. The men pulled it in at a landing, and they walked the horses off. Then the hard poling began again.

The landing was called Nestor, after the town several miles inland alongside Nestor Creek. When they rode in, they found the place bursting its seams with people who had come from the surrounding countryside to the fair. Henry grinned at the banner: County Fair! Banners and bunting were strung everywhere, even across the main street. Everyone they saw was in a gala mood.

The hotel was filled and every available space occupied, including the stable. It was the first big entertainment in that part of the state for years, the clerk told them, and people were making the most of it.

The livery had rented out stalls also, but most people were sleeping in wagons—or under them—out in the open fields, cooking over campfires.

They had no choice but to do the same ... without a wagon or tent. Looking at all the campfires that night, the general was reminded of the war.

In the morning they roamed about the meadows, looking at the hundreds of objects and vegetables on display. In one field were pens of animals to be judged, in another were small shedlike buildings where enterprising concessionaires had set up business, each one shouting the virtues of his wares or the chances to be taken. An oval track had also been laid out, and there would be races later in the day. A gang of men was still building seats for spectators along the main stretch.

But wonder of wonders, there was a hot air balloon, tugging at its mooring! A sign in front of it read: "Prof. H. R. Roddins, Balloonist. Each ascent 50¢ per person."

The general was fascinated by the prospect, saying he wanted to go up. Balloons had been used by the Union army in the late war, McRae said, by a Professor Lowe, and had been successful in spying out Confederate troop movements.

McRae talked to the professor, asking him how he kept the air hot in the balloon, and was shown the arrangement, which Roddins said he had invented himself. It was a coal brazier in a cast-iron pot, with a tall chimney leading up into the balloon's interior.

"With coal there's no danger of sparks," the professor said. "And as long as there's fuel to burn, the balloon will stay up. Without it, the balloon will gradually cool and drift to earth."

"I've heard that some balloonists use hydrogen gas."

"Yes, but it's far more expensive than hot air, and very much more dangerous. If it ignites—poof! Up you go, balloon and all, in a torch!"

"Speaking of up, how far up do you go?"

"Only to the end of the rope, about a hundred feet. In free flight the balloon will go up several thousand, of course. It gets surprisingly cold high up."

"Cold? Closer to the sun?"

"Yes. Curious, isn't it?"

There was a windlass on a heavy base, which the professor pointed out. It allowed the balloon to ascend to the end of the rope, then it was pulled down by the professor's assistants, who worked the hand cranks that were geared to a large drum around which the rope was wound.

The balloon, a large, bulbous shape, slowly filling, moved sluggishly in the still air. It would take awhile before it would be ready to go up, the professor said.

The general promised he would be back, and they walked on. On a kind of bulletin board, contests were announced: plowing, shucking corn . . . and shooting. First prize for pistol shooting was twenty-five dollars. McRae urged Slocum to enter.

There had been no sign of their enemies; crossing the river had possibly left them far behind. How would a pursuer guess they were attending a local fair? Slocum assented and put up the entry fee. He was one of about forty men eager for the prize.

Half of them were eliminated very quickly.

Targets were drawn with paint on heavy paper tacked to wooden frames, which were twenty-five paces away with backstops of baled hay. Half of those shooters left were whittled down to ten in half an hour. Then the targets were reduced in size and each man given three shots.

When those shots were examined by the two judges, only three men were left, and Slocum was one of them.

The second was a pudgy man with thick fingers. He wore tattered jeans, a woolen shirt, and a perpetual smile.

The third was an old-timer in buckskin shirt and pants. He and Slocum were firing Navy Colts. The pudgy man used a Remington and was eliminated in the next round. One of his shots was a quarter of an inch out.

Slocum faced the old-timer, who said his name was Larson. It was announced that each man would fire five shots, and the contest would be concluded. The best shot group would win. They flipped a coin; Larson won the selection and decided to fire first.

He fired his five rounds very slowly and deliberately, taking his time. When he finished, one of the judges walked out and brought back the target.

Slocum smiled at McRae and Henry, stepped to the firing line, and fired his five, also taking his time.

When the judge walked out and brought back the target, there was a conference between the two. Slocum's target showed that only four shots had hit it. Had he missed the target entirely? It did not seem likely. Then one of the judges brought out a magnifying glass, and they both studied the target again.

Two of the bullets had gone through the same hole! The glass showed that one hole was slightly enlarged.

Slocum was awarded the prize.

Hidden by trees, Stark and Charlie Bannon watched the flatboat cross the river. They could not see the faces of the men aboard, but the three horses were plain as the nose on a democrat.

"It's them right enough," Stark said. "We've got to get across. We'd best go back to Norton Springs. There's plenty boats there."

There were a dozen boats to choose from at the waterfront. They got the horses aboard one and were taken across, then asked about the next town.

"It's Nestor," the boatman replied. "Three, four hours down. You'll see the landing." He grinned, showing gap teeth. "Take you there f' two more dollars."

"We'll ride," Stark said shortly. Two dollars for a few hours on a boat!

The boatman was right; it took them four hours to reach the Nestor Landing . . . to discover the town was inland. It was dark when they arrived, but the street was gay with bunting and colored lanterns. Musicians were playing and people dancing in the square; the fair was going full blast.

They ate in a crowded restaurant, then wandered through the crowds, looking for the three men. Had they come here? There was no one to ask.

Like dozens of others, they rolled up in their blankets on the grass.

The next morning they waited outside the restaurant for a table, then wandered through the crowds again. Stark began to be sure the three had gone on. What would keep them here?

Then he saw the balloon. He had heard of them but had never seen one before. It was round as a turnip, dark red in color, with a kind of rope netting over it and other ropes holding a big square basket that was several feet off the ground.

There was a stepladder beside the basket and a man climbing up into it.

The man was General McRae!

11

McRae had expressed the desire to make a balloon ascent, and so they returned—in time to hear Professor Roddins explaining to half a dozen listeners that there was no possible danger involved in going up in his balloon.

But the audience seemed unmoved. No one offered to buy a ticket.

Terra firma was one thing, a man said, and the sky quite another. What if the big red bag went up and disappeared in the clouds? What then, Professor?

Roddins answered all the queries in a reasonable voice and, when his listeners still kept their money in their pockets, announced that he alone would make an ascent to prove to them that it was as safe as sitting in a church on Sunday.

He spoke to his two burly assistants and climbed up into the basket.

McRae hurried up and called out that he would like to go along. The professor smiled and extended a helping hand.

At that moment, as the general put a leg over to get into the basket, a shot sounded and a bullet *spang*ed off the iron chimney. Slocum turned, drawing the Colt as more shots were fired at the balloon. He knew instantly that he could not get the general out of the basket in safety. The only course was to get him out of reach.

Two horsemen were doing the firing, and he snapped shots at them as he ran and jumped at the basket, clambering up. He shouted at the professor to let the rope go, and got in front of the general, firing again at the two horsemen. Was one of them the squinty-eyed man?

With admirable presence of mind, Roddins released the rope that held them down, and the balloon soared upward. More shots came, plunking into the sandbags that were strung along the sides of the basket.

Down below, people were scurrying in every direction like ants. Henry Biggs was standing, shading his eyes, looking up at them. The two horsemen were galloping to follow the balloon.

Turning, Slocum asked the general if he was hit, and McRae shook his head.

Roddins said in a sour voice, "What the hell was that? Who was shooting?"

"Someone's after us," Slocum said. "How high will this balloon go?"

"Only a hundred feet."

"That's not high enough. A rifle will reach us easily at that height. Cut the rope."

When Roddins hesitated, Slocum said, "They'll cut this basket to ribbons and us, too. You want that?"

Roddins sighed and shook his head. He drew a clasp knife and sawed the rope through.

The balloon moved faster as the rope dropped away. The ground receded; people became smaller and smaller.

And the professor was annoyed. "How long will we have to stay up here?"

"We're out of rifle range now," Slocum said in relief. "And we're drifting eastward . . ."

"I asked you—"

McRae said gently, "I expect we could come down after dark. What do you say, John?"

Slocum nodded, gazing down.

"You've put me out of business, you two. You know that."

"I'll make it up to you," McRae said. "Tell me what you've lost . . ."

Slocum stared around them. The ground seemed hardly to move down there. He had never in the world expected to be in a balloon basket high above mother earth this way. It was a frightening yet glorious experience! He could see for miles in every direction. To the west was the shimmering river. The town, which was slowly fading into the distance, was composed of dolls' houses. The wagons he could see were toys.

He looked around as the professor added coals to the brazier. Roddins said, "We'll have to come down in a few hours. We don't have enough fuel. Off the ground the balloon cools rapidly. But if we're lucky, we'll find ourselves near a town."

McRae gazed up at the dark red bag. "There's no way you can steer it, I suppose . . . ?"

"No. None. We're at a mercy of the winds." The professor wetted a finger and held it up. "No wind at the moment . . . hardly any."

"We're not moving fast," McRae observed.

"Speed is deceptive at this altitude. We'll be miles from the fairgrounds when we land. Let's pray we don't get caught in some wild windstream. If we do, it'll carry us a hundred miles in an hour."

"Is that possible?"

"Oh, yes. It happens. I've often suspected that the sky has as many currents as the ocean." Roddins smiled. "Maybe one day someone will ride a balloon across the Atlantic."

McRae shook his head. "You're a dreamer, sir."

"I think it's possible." The professor shrugged. "A much larger balloon than this, of course."

• • •

Seeing the general climb into the balloon basket, Stark yanked out his pistol and fired, oblivious of the crowd. He nudged the horse and thumbed back the hammer on the revolver, seeing the big man, Slocum, turn toward him. He fired again at the balloon and galloped the horse in a circle as Charlie fired at the air bag. Around him, people were yelling and running, startled by the shooting.

Then Slocum leaped up, caught the rim of the basket, and heaved himself over. Stark fired again and again, emptying the pistol at the basket.

Someone on the ground was firing at him, and he put spurs to the horse. He saw the balloon shoot upward and swore. He and Charlie galloped past the concession shacks, out of the fairground meadows. They had caused a mighty ruckus, and the local law would be after them in a hurry unless they made tracks.

They came onto a rutted road that led eastward, and Stark turned into it at once. They galloped for a mile or more, then Stark halted in an open area and looked for the balloon. It was high in the sky—someone had cut the tether rope. It looked to be a mile up. He swore again; that damned Slocum!

"It's driftin' toward east," Charlie said. "You want us to foller it?"

Stark growled and nodded, and they set out again with Stark keeping one eye on the travelers in the sky. How long could the damned thing stay up?

In a few miles the road bent north, and they left it and continued cross-country, moving slower. The balloon drifted ahead of them, gradually becoming smaller in the clear sky.

"We goin' to lose it," Charlie said. "Can they fly at night?"

"Why not?"

Charlie made a face and grinned. "I don't know much about balloons. You figger they got any grub with 'em?"

Stark whistled. That was something he hadn't thought of. They would have to come down to eat!

The professor allowed the big red air bag to cool gradually as evening approached. They would be able to see the sun, he told them, long after it had disappeared from those on the ground.

As the air in the balloon cooled, the bag slowly settled to earth. A town had appeared in the distance, and the professor did his best to keep them up so they would land near it. There were too many trees, so he picked an open space and was able to come down there. The basket hit with a bump and dragged thirty or forty feet in the grass, then the air bag folded and crumpled like a huge wounded beast . . . but they were down.

They clambered out of the basket, and Slocum asked, "How far do you think we are from the fair?"

"Forty miles?" McRae guessed.

Professor Roddins shook his head. "More like double that. As I told you, speed is deceptive in a balloon high up." He gazed toward the town they'd seen from above. "I'd guess the town is about five miles away. You can go in, but I'll have to stay here with the balloon."

"No one knows it's here . . ."

"Horses could trample the balloon and ruin it. I'll stay here and fold it. Will you send a man with a wagon to pick me up? I want to return to the fair as soon as possible. Everything I own is there."

"Of course," McRae said. "You may have to sleep here."

Roddins nodded. "I've slept in the basket before."

They set out across the fields on foot, but it took three hours to reach the town, and it was dark by then. The little town was at a crossroads. A store, trading post, and blacksmith shop joined with a few other stores, a cluster of houses, and a straggle of shacks by a spring that had formed a small pond. According to a sign on the trading post, it was called Tupin.

The general store had a side room that was a saloon. A half dozen men were sitting at tables, drinking and arguing over cards. They stared curiously at the newcomers who asked if there was a place to stay overnight in the town.

"We ain't got a hotel," the owner said. "We don't get us much travelin' folks."

One of the card players said, "Miz Keene has took in boarders now'n then."

Slocum said, "We also need a wagon and a driver."

"Try the blacksmith. He's got a couple wagons."

"Thanks. Where's Mrs. Keene's place?"

The owner went to the door and pointed to the house. "The one with the maple tree in front. Tell her Josiah sent y'all."

"Thank you," the general said.

Mrs. Keene was a slim woman in a high-necked dress. She was thirty-five or so, Slocum thought, and not at all bad looking; he had expected to see a dowdy fat housewife. She welcomed them, hearing Josiah's name. She had a large house, and since her husband had died, it was really too large, and she was seriously thinking of moving back to St. Louis, where she had kin. Yes, indeed. She could put them up for the night.

Slocum walked back to the blacksmith's shop, finding it closed. He rapped on the door behind the shop, and a big black-haired man came out. Slocum said howdy and explained about the wagon and driver. "It has to go back to Nestor."

"That's a good trip. Are you going with it?"

"No. The man who needs the wagon is five miles west. Can you handle it—if the pay is right?"

The smith grinned, showing large square teeth. "I c'n handle anything if the pay is right."

"That's a good attitude," Slocum said. "The man's name is Professor Roddins and he's guarding a balloon and a basket."

"Jesus! A balloon?"

"That's right. We flew here from Nestor, and now he's got to get back."

"The wind blowed you here, huh? I never seen a balloon."

"I never did either," Slocum confessed, "until yesterday. Then I went up in the damned thing."

"Yeah? How was it?"

"Amazing. You can see all the way to China. If you haul the professor back to Nestor, I'm sure he will take you up."

"Not me, he won't. I'll send one of my boys along."

Slocum made the deal, giving the blacksmith some of Reardon's money and directions to find Roddins in the field. The smith promised he would have the wagon there first thing in the morning.

Slocum returned to the Keene house and found the general sitting in the parlor with Mrs. Keene, sipping coffee . . . with a little brandy. She was fixing to make supper for them, she said, and Slocum smiled. McRae had obviously charmed her to the bone.

The sprawling home had a large bedroom, occupied by Mrs. Keene, and three small ones on the opposite side of the house. Slocum's room had a narrow bed, a chair, and a washstand. There was a carpet on the floor and curtains on the single window. The general's room was two doors away, with a deep closet in between.

He washed his face and combed his hair, and they sat down to supper. The general talked about New Orleans before the war, the theater parties and the races . . . Mrs. Keene said it was the most delightful dinner they'd ever had in the house. She served them tender beef and yams and even brought out an apple pie for dessert, which the general declared was the best pie he had ever eaten.

In the tiny bedroom Slocum shucked his clothes and slipped into bed naked, glad to be indoors again. He thought of the professor, sleeping in the open basket, and shook his head ruefully. Nothing he could do about that.

The room was dark when he blew out the lamp. He lay back on the pillow with a sigh and closed his eyes . . . and heard the door open. It was only the faintest click.

He reached for his revolver.

12

Emily Keene's voice said softly, "You won't need that." She closed the door behind her and moved toward him to sit on the edge of the bed.

"Are you comfortable, John Slocum?"

"Very," he said, smiling in the gloom.

"Are you married?"

"No."

"Neither am I."

He chuckled and pushed back the covers. This was a very unusual woman. He said, "There's room for two—barely."

She slid into bed and pulled up the covers as his arms went about her. She was wearing almost nothing. She murmured something as he embraced her, then slipped off the lacy gown she wore and tossed it to a chair.

He looked down at her in the shadowy room and she was smiling. "Another week and I would have missed you."

He brushed her lips with his. "You're going to St. Louis then?"

"Yes. The house here is sold."

"Are you going looking for a husband?"

She laughed softly. "Maybe. Is that so terrible? If I find one I'll accept him gratefully. But there are other reasons. This little town is stifling, you know. Sometimes I think its main business is gossip."

"Did you come in here tonight to tell me that?"

She laughed softly again and their lips met. He moved over her and she guided him, and they said nothing more for a long time . . . He was mildly surprised that the bed did not squeak, nor did the headboard pound the wall.

He was asleep when she slid out of the bed and left the room. In the morning it was as if the night before had not happened. She made breakfast, and when they were about to go the general brought out money and settled up with her, then kissed her hand. She looked at Slocum and smiled.

They walked to the stable, and Slocum paused at the wide, open doors and looked back. She was still standing on the porch, looking after them. He waved, sighed, and went into the stable.

They bought horses and saddles and a sack of canned food from the store and were on their way south long before midday. There was no road and they navigated by guess. The great river was somewhere to the west, and they edged that way. It was difficult to use the sun as a guide at noon, but if it went down in the west as usual that night, it would be a help.

Buford Stark and Charlie followed the disappearing balloon. It went out of sight, but Stark knew it had to continue on the same path, barring unexpected high winds, and it had to come down sometime.

In due course they stumbled onto Tupin and made the usual inquiries. Had three strangers on foot come into the town very recently?

No. But two had. Stark described the general to the store owner.

"Yea, he was one of 'em."

The stableman said he had sold them horses.

If they had bought horses they had not continued in the balloon.

Stark and Charlie headed south.

When they came to shining railroad tracks, Slocum turned to follow them southwest. The rails were paralleled by a line of telegraph poles. Wire and tracks led them to Cherry Hill.

The town was at the end of the track, a spur line. There was a small depot and telegraph office, several sidings where a few weathered boxcars waited, and several corrals beside the tracks. The town was on a single main street wide enough for wagons to be parked in the center, and there was a hotel advertising hot baths for twenty-five cents.

They signed for rooms, and the general went to the bathhouse immediately. Slocum walked to the telegraph office.

He sent wires to Reardon and Munch, saying they were heading north and expected to be back in Norton Springs in three or four days. If someone was reading their wires who should not, that ought to cause confusion.

Returning to the hotel, he had a bath and a shave. Over supper he told McRae what he had done, and the general smiled.

"Then we should have no further trouble."

"We're a long way from New Orleans, sir."

"What about Henry Biggs?"

"He'll get another job," Slocum said. "One without shooting connected to it . . . I hope."

"Yes. Let's hope so."

In the morning they left the town behind. They followed a road south for several hours, until it forked. They took the west fork and came to a wide stream that barred further progress westward. It curved south and they went along with it. The land was wild; they saw no houses, and there were no paths or trails except those made by animals.

When they finally approached a settlement, it was only a wide place in the road—what road there was, a trail leading into it from the south. There was a store, a deadfall and three houses, a dozen shacks, and some corrals, all hunched up by the stream on a high bank. A forested area pushed against it from the east, and even from a distance, Slocum could see the place was poor as a broken-down mule.

He said quietly, "Look at your caps, General."

He pulled his own pistol and examined it as McRae did the same.

"You expect trouble, John?"

Slocum shrugged. "They may think we're richer than they are—some of them. It's wise to take precautions."

"Of course."

"We'll go into the store together and stay close. All right?"

"I'll follow your lead. Where do you suppose we are?"

"No idea. I think that balloon drifted farther than even the professor thought."

"I think so, too."

The buildings of the settlement were set down in haphazard fashion. There was no street as such, and no fences. There was a hitch rack in front of the store, which had a crudely lettered sign: "Larkin Store Gen'l Merch."

They got down in front, looking about them. Everything looked peaceful; even the dogs in the street yawned at them. A man sitting in front of the next-door deadfall got up and went inside as Slocum eyed him. He glanced at the sky; it was the middle of the afternoon.

He followed McRae into the store. Three men were talking near the back, one probably the store owner—he wore a dirty white apron. All three looked at them in surprise, as if they might have come from the moon.

Slocum nodded at them in friendly fashion. "What d'you call this place?"

"I guess we calls it Larkins," the man with the apron said.

"Are you Mr. Larkin?"

"Nope. Larkin, he up and died five year ago. I bought the store from 'is widow." He moved behind the littered counter. "You ain't lawmen, are you?"

Slocum's brows went up. "No. We're just passing through, heading west."

"You ain't been here b'fore?"

"Never. How far is the river, would you say?"

"Thirty-forty mile. But there ain't no road."

McRae smiled. "Not many roads in this part of the country, sir." He laid the empty gunnysack on the counter.

They bought airtights, coffee, and matches. As the owner got them down from the shelves, the two men who had been talking to him sidled out. One had a pronounced limp; the other was hatless and had red hair. Neither looked prosperous.

They paid the owner, tied on the food sack, and rode out past the houses and corrals. A nuzzling of mules studied them, and chickens scattered from their path. In minutes they were in the pine woods.

Out of sight of the buildings, Slocum turned left at once. The men who lived in the settlement knew every inch of the ground, of course; if they were of a mind, they had probably picked out a good ambush spot, hoping their prospective victims would continue westward as they had started.

If they were of a killing mind.

And if they were, how long would they wait in that spot? Doubtless not long. Soon they would send someone to see where the pilgrims had gone.

"You still think we're in danger?" McRae asked.

"I do. Yes. I wish I knew how many of them there were."

"Three or four?"

"A good guess."

They walked the horses through the woods, an old forest with fallen trees everywhere and thick brush. They came abruptly to a plowed field and skirted it, then a huge marshy area that smelled abominably. In an hour they forded a small stream and halted to let the horses drink.

Rifle shots cracked by them suddenly—by the sounds, from a distance.

Slocum spurred into the trees after the general. "They're mad as hell! They should have waited to get closer."

McRae nodded, grinning. "We didn't do what they expected."

"Yes. They've got the advantage now, though. They know the country. We could get boxed in somewhere if we're unlucky. I think our best bet is to ride directly away from them." He was also thinking that an unlucky shot could hit the general.

McRae said, "Lead on."

Slocum headed into the trees; they were ash and hackberry for the most part. There was little brush, and they were able to move in a relatively straight line for several miles and thus make better time. At long intervals a few scattered shots came after them, rapping into trees or screaming into the sky, doing no harm at all. The pursuers were letting off steam.

Slocum wondered how far they would chase. It probably depended on how hungry they were for loot. Of course, the two horses were worth something . . .

In an hour they were in foothills, climbing through a narrow canyon that twisted and turned. They were also leaving plain tracks, and nothing they could do about it but hope that darkness would conceal them.

The canyon branched half a dozen times in the next few miles, small dead ends mostly. They were not high hills, and Slocum worried that their pursuers knew a way around or would come over the crests, but they did not do that. When they came to a more definite branch that led westward, they took it, and the canyon widened at once and became sandy.

But there was less cover; the trees were scattered and more stunted. They followed no trail; it did not look as if anyone had ever been there. And the sun was going down. In another hour the western slopes were in deep shadow. And as the light faded, a few shots, fired from long distances, came seeking them out, the echoes crashing amid the steep canyon walls.

The pursuers had no real hope of hitting anything, Slocum thought. They were probably letting off steam, expressing their feelings. Probably they expected the night to help them.

The canyon widened, and shallow ravines appeared as the land changed, clotted with brittle brown brush and low growth. Looking back, Slocum saw they were leaving less of a trail as the ground hardened, and when night descended, he turned eastward abruptly and they walked the horses, traversing winding ravines, making as little sound as possible.

When they halted for a breather McRae asked, "D'you think we've lost them?"

"Maybe—until morning. If they've got a tracker with them they'll be on the trail quickly."

"Let's hope they don't."

They ate cold beans from cans and went on slowly, picking their way in the dark and, after a mile or so, turned south again in a wide wash.

In a few hours the wash narrowed and deepened. The banks on either side were five and six feet high and shadowy. The wash was sandy and pebbled, with large boulders here and there, and it became more and more difficult to make their way. Slocum halted and suggested they wait for dawn. McRae agreed and got down tiredly.

Slocum took the first watch—and let the general sleep. He woke the other when the first hints of daybreak began to sweep across the eastern sky, and they went on. Slocum looked for a way out of the wash, but the sides were too steep for the horses to climb. The wash also began to make a series of turns, as if unable to make up its mind. And as they approached one of those, Slocum halted abruptly and backed his horse, motioning urgently to McRae.

A half dozen shots came, slamming into the canyon wall, causing tiny avalanches. Slocum slid off the horse and hugged the wall. "They got ahead of us—three or four of 'em."

McRae led the horses farther back. "How did you know they were there?"

"I saw one of 'em move. They're behind some rocks." He looked at the sky. "We may have to go back to get out of this damned wash."

"How do you suppose they got ahead of us?"

"Because they know the country—and maybe they made some good guesses."

"I'm surprised they're so determined."

Slocum nodded. "It means they're hungry. And that'll make them vicious. They want whatever we've got." He glanced up again. The sun was beginning to flush the sky. He edged forward, taking off his hat, and studied the distant rocks. He could see several men moving there, possibly discussing the odds on a charge, now that they were so close.

He drew the Navy and motioned for the general to mount. Maybe he could discourage them a bit. They were within long range. Aiming carefully, he fired three times at them, unable to tell if he had hit any. They fired back instantly, raising dust.

Slocum mounted, and they rode back the way they had come.

He shoved linen cartridges into the three cylinders, tamped them down, and recapped the nipples. He swore under his breath. The chase was getting serious, and the general, though he never complained, was obviously very near exhaustion.

When they came to a long straight stretch, more shots came from far behind, rifles at long distance. None reached them.

In an hour they found a way out of the wash and were on up-slanting land covered with brown grass and wildflowers in swaths. Slocum led directly away from the wash, heading west. They went over the crest of a gentle hill and along the foothills of a sharp ridge. No shots followed them.

Slocum said, "With a little luck they won't notice where we climbed out of the wash, and go past it. That might gain us an hour."

"Are they going to chase us all the way to New Orleans?"

Slocum chuckled. "What else do they have to do?"

The general sighed. "Sometimes I wish I had never written those memoirs . . ."

"Or told anyone about them."

McRae nodded. "Yes. That too. It was a terrible mistake."

13

The hills began to level out, and in two hours they were in a pine forest, moving slowly with Slocum in the lead. The trees were thick, and he could not see a hundred feet ahead, nor see the sky. It was difficult to move in a straight line. They paused at a stream to drink and let the horses drink. It was getting late in the day.

Then the trees thinned out and they came to a small clearing. As they entered it, a fusillade of shots came from the far side. Powder smoke erupted from the brush, and the general's horse reared.

Slocum's pistol was out and firing in a second. He heard the general firing as he jumped clear of the horse that fell, legs kicking. Slocum spurred and grabbed McRae, yelling to him to grab the horn—and galloped back into the trees with bullets cracking past like vicious bees.

The general's horse was dead. McRae was untouched, and Slocum got down and examined his mount, finding no wounds. But this put them at a great disadvantage. They had lost the horse, half their food, and the general's blanket roll.

He mounted again and pulled McRae up behind him.

They moved on, watching for pursuit. Had they hit any of them? He had emptied his revolver, six shots into the brush. And he had twenty-five dollars' prize money to prove he could shoot straight.

But no one came after them.

After a few minutes Slocum halted. McRae said, "What is it?"

"They've been following us for two days, and they've never been so close before. Where are they?"

"Maybe we hurt them. We both fired at them—and you were closer."

Slocum nodded. "I'm going back."

"Is that wise?" McRae slid off the horse.

Slocum dismounted and handed the reins over. "I'm getting tired of being chased. Stay here, General. I won't be long."

He moved into the trees, walking on matted pine needles whenever possible. He was probably a mile from the little clearing, and he made a circle to come up on it from the west, moving cautiously from tree to tree, the pistol in his hand.

He found where their horses had been picketed. And at the edge of the clearing, he nearly stumbled on two bodies. One was the redhaired man he'd seen in the store, the other an older man with a scraggly beard. Red Hair had been hit just above the ear; the other had taken two bullets in the chest.

Someone had gone through their pockets and also taken the weapons . . . and the horses. But he had not been able to bury the bodies.

Slocum looked for tracks and found them; the trail headed north, crossing the open space. It looked to him like the tracks of three horses. If so, one man had survived and was going home . . . poorer, Slocum hoped, and sadder. Maybe a little wiser.

He debated going after the man—they had a good debt to pay him—but when he returned to the general and they discussed it, the general advised forgetting it.

There was nothing they could do about the bodies either. The general picked up his blanket roll and food sack, climbed up behind Slocum, and they pointed west.

The land became less creased and hilly, and the next morning they saw smoke in the distance. It came from a farmhouse surrounded by maples and oaks.

The farmer's wife and two small children were home. Her husband was in the fields with their bigger sons, she told them. Yes, they had several horses, but she didn't know if they would be for sale.

Leaving the general behind, Slocum rode out to the field where the farmer was harrowing. The man was lean, dark haired, and dull eyed. His sons were in the next field with a mule team. Did he have a horse for sale? He considered, looking Slocum over. Slocum mentioned cash, hard money, and the man nodded. He decided he had a two-year-old bay he could let go. They walked back to the barn, and the farmer brought out the horse.

Slocum and the general looked her over, a mare with a long black tail. She had been recently shod, and she seemed in perfect condition.

"She's gentle," the farmer said. "M' boys been a-ridin' her to school over to Edgerton. That's four, five mile south."

McRae asked, "Don't they go to school any longer?"

"They thirteen and fourteen. They work here now. Got no need for school."

"How about a saddle?" Slocum asked.

The farmer shook his head. "Alls I got is a hackamore you welcome to. But you can maybe pick up a saddle in Edgerton if you's goin' that way."

The general wrote out a bill of sale and the farmer signed it, proud that he could write his name. He tossed a blanket into the deal, and McRae climbed on the bay horse with only the blanket to ease the trip.

There was a road of sorts, but the town was mostly closed up when they arrived after dark. The liveryman sold them a well-worn saddle and a bridle and let them sleep in one of the stalls—the town had no hotel. The river, he told them, was thirty miles to the west, give or take . . .

The river had been much closer when he was a boy, he said. "But it took off. The damn river is allus movin' . . . and floodin'. We had a neighbor lost 'is whole farm one spring. The river ate it."

"How far's the next town?" Slocum asked.

" 'Bout a day's ride west."

"Is there a hotel?"

The stableman scratched his head. "I dunno. I never been there."

They took a well-rutted road that wound through the countryside, taking the path of least resistance, and reached the town, Yaleburg, at dusk. There was a hotel, and McRae fell into bed, exhausted.

Buford Stark received a wire that said the general should be in Norton Springs.

He said to Charlie, "They went back upriver."

"Tryin' to throw us off."

"I suppose so . . ."

Immediately they headed north. It took four days to return to the town, and they learned in the first few hours that no one had seen the general or Slocum—or said they had not.

Charlie wondered, "Maybe we got here ahead of 'em?"

"Maybe so." Stark sent another wire and received an answer. No other wire had been received from Slocum. At last report the general was in Norton Springs or heading for it. The wire suggested Stark wait for him.

He waited three days, then sent another wire. The general was definitely not in the town. Something must have happened to keep him from it. Or the sender's information was wrong.

The return wire suggested he do something constructive instead of sitting in a hotel.

Stark sighed deeply and went to the waterfront. He hired a boat and started visiting river towns.

The general slept the clock around and got up wearily the next evening, hungry as a bear. The restaurant was open, so he and Slocum went across the street and had supper.

Over coffee Slocum asked, "Do you feel like going on in the morning?"

"Oh yes. A little rest was all I needed."

"Good."

They went back to the hotel and played cards for an hour or two. McRae was not sleepy. He bought several newspapers and went to his room on the first floor. Slocum went upstairs to his room and went to bed.

In the morning he went downstairs and rapped on the general's door. There was no answer. Probably McRae had gotten up early and maybe gone to breakfast. He asked at the desk but the clerk said, "I just come on—I ain't seen him."

He went across to the restaurant, but McRae was not there either.

However, his horse was in the hotel stable.

He asked the clerk to open McRae's room, and it was as if the general had left it only moments before. Nothing was disturbed. His blanket roll and gun were on a chair, his soap and razor on the washstand.

Where the hell was he? Was it possible the sharp-nosed man had found and spirited him away?

The stableman had not seen him—but the town marshal had. McRae was in jail!

Marshal R. J. Eddins was a portly man with a drooping gray mustache and agate-hard eyes. He sat in a battered chair behind his littered desk and stared at Slocum when he entered. A deputy across the room was cleaning a shotgun.

"He's in jail?" Slocum said incredulously. "What for?"

Eddins shoved a Wanted dodger across the desk. "That him?"

Slocum picked it up. Wanted for Murder. He gazed at the tintype of a lean-faced man who vaguely resembled the general as he might have been ten years or more past. He shook his head. "No. That's not him."

The marshal grunted. He took the poster back and frowned at it. "Can't take the chance it ain't." He squinted at Slocum. "What you doin' with him?"

"We're traveling together."

"You knowed him long?"

"No, not long. Are you thinking of locking me up, too?"

Eddins made a face. "You ain't wanted, far's I know."

"Marshal, the man you've got in jail is Butler McRae, a lawyer and a former Confederate general officer."

"General, hey!" Eddins whistled. "You hear that, Jed? We got us a general in our caboose." He looked back at Slocum, his hard eyes narrowed. "I was for the Union m'self."

"You're making a mistake, Marshal. This man is no crook."

"We'll see about that."

"How long are you going to hold him?"

Eddins grunted again. "We got to hold him till the circuit judge gits here."

"How long will that be?"

"A month. Maybe two months. Hard to tell. That all you wanted to know?" He motioned toward the door.

Slocum went back to the hotel stable and rubbed down both horses, for something to do. This was as big a nuisance as it was unexpected. One or two months in a drafty little crackerbox jail was likely to undermine the general's health. They would probably feed him turnips and gravy and treat him worse.

He walked up and down the alley behind the hotel, worrying about it. They would hold McRae until the circuit judge appeared—and of course the judge was certain to release him. But a month or more would have passed.

Also there was a good chance the news of his arrest would be published, if only in a local paper. But their enemies might see it...

What should he do?

14

Should he break McRae out? If he did, then the law would be on their trail as well as sharp-nose and his bunch. The local marshal's jurisdiction probably went no farther than the end of town. But wouldn't he notify every sheriff in the land?

Slocum paced and kicked stones. He could not leave the general in that damned jail for even a week—no matter the consequences. He had to get him out.

That decided, he felt better. Now—how should he go about it?

He went back and looked at the jail building again. It was weathered boards with a shingle roof, like most of the other buildings in town. It was a jail built to hold weekend drunks, not hardened criminals who might have a gang ready to take on the entire town. The marshal's office faced the street, with the jail in back. Slocum could see only a few high-up windows, all on the ground floor. There was no second story.

What if he set it afire? The unpainted wood would burn like a torch. It might set off other buildings near it. In fact, the entire town might burn. Small wooden towns were always burning to the ground, because heat and light depended so often on open fires.

But if he did that, he might burn up the general, too. He was in a locked cell, after all. No . . . better forget fire.

Probably the best way would be to go in late at night with a six-gun. Chances were that only one guard would be on duty through the night. He made small talk with the hotel clerk and learned that Marshal Eddins had only one deputy, Jed. And the marshal was heavy in the butt and slept in his own bed at home while he let Jed use the office cot when he had prisoners in the cells.

So, he would face only one sleepy man.

Slocum perused a map of the area and decided their best escape route was north. There was a much-traveled road leading south to the next town, and they might be expected to take it. Of course, at night the law would not be able to study tracks until dawn. That would give him and McRae several hours' start.

The bad news was that it was Friday. Friday and Saturday were blow-off-steam nights. The saloons were full, and drunks were hauled off to the pokey when they made a nuisance of themselves on the street. Both the marshal and Jed worked very late, making rounds and settling the town down each night.

Slocum bought a crowbar in the general store. Monday was ideal, he thought. Both lawmen were tired, and all the drunks had been set loose in the morning, sobered up and fined. He watched the portly marshal leave the office and tramp wearily to his home close by.

When he walked past the jail, Slocum could see the deputy inside alone. He went back to the hotel and slept for several hours.

Near midnight he got up and dressed, left money on the bed to pay for the room rent, and went down the back steps to the stable.

Stark and Charlie went from one river town to the next, looking and asking questions. Then they crossed the river after about fifty miles and went upstream doing the same.

They found no trace of the general and his bodyguard.

"They got to be somewhere," Charlie said. "They ain't on the river."

"That balloon went a long way. Maybe they're somewhere in between—if they came back toward the river."

"That's a hell of a lot of country to look at . . ."

Stark sighed deeply. It certainly was. And at that point he debated giving it all up. It was like hunting a button in a mudhole. But, he was being well paid. And he might not do as well if he cut himself loose . . .

He decided to mull it over and try again. Where in hell could they be?

Leading McRae's horse, Slocum rode down the alley a dozen minutes past midnight. The town was dark and silent; most were asleep. Many went to bed soon after dark as a rule anyway. What was there to do, sitting up—play checkers? Probably not five people in town, he thought, had stayed up till midnight in ten years. The night clerk in the hotel had been asleep on a cot behind the desk.

He turned into the dark street; the town had no streetlights at all. Probably no town west of Cincinnati had them, and even the saloons were closed. Stepping down in front of the jail, he tried the door. Locked. Glancing around, he slid the sharp end of the crowbar between the door and the jamb and pulled. The lock gave way with a snap. There was a soft splintering of wood and the door was open.

Slocum walked in with the Colt in his hand as the groggy deputy said, "What the hell . . ."

Pulling the hammer back on the revolver, a deadly *click-clack*, Slocum said, "Just stay quiet."

He struck a match. Jed blinked at him from the cot; he looked into the muzzle of the gun. "What you want?"

"The general. Light a lamp."

Jed slid out of the cot in his John Ls, struck another match, lifted the glass chimney, and lighted the wick.

Slocum said, "Pick up your clothes and walk into the cells." Jed's gun was on the desk and he left it there. He took the jail keys, which were on a large metal ring, and followed the deputy.

There were four cells, two very large and two small. McRae was sleeping in one of the smaller. Slocum handed Jed the keys. "Unlock the door and wake him."

Jed nodded. "The marshal's gonna be mad as hell in the morning."

"I suppose so. Wake him."

The general was astonished, looking from Jed in his underwear to Slocum with a cocked pistol. "Well, hello, John!"

"Get dressed, General. We're getting out of here."

McRae pulled on his clothes, and Jed sat down on the bunk. "You going to lock me in?"

"Sorry. But we have to. It'll be better for you anyway. No sense you getting shot over a simple jailbreak."

Jed managed a weak smile.

They rode out of town slowly and head north over dark fields under a starless sky. A heavy mist was settling in and it was chilly. Summer was going fast.

Slocum said, "I talked to the marshal and he told me it would be a month or more until the circuit judge showed up to try your case. So I decided that was too long."

"I see. But of course now we're fugitives. He'll wire every town on the telegraph to be on the lookout for us, won't he?"

"Yes, I expect so. But you didn't want to stay in that jail, did you?"

McRae laughed. "No, I certainly did not!"

"Then we'll take our chances."

McRae glanced around. "We're not going south, are we?"

"No, we're heading north. It's a simple deception. I think they'll expect us to go south on the road. We mentioned south in the hotel, and the marshal will ask about us there."

"I'm sure he will."

They rode all night and toward morning came onto a trail that led westward. When the sun came up they saw there was no sign of wheeled traffic on it. The track led them to a cluster of farm buildings. They halted, examining the far-off buildings with the general's binoculars.

"Better go around," Slocum advised.

They made a wide circle, avoiding contact. Miles from the houses Slocum dug a deep hole and made a small fire to boil coffee. They ate from the cans, then went on into a pine forest.

They were still wending their way through the trees in late afternoon. Then they halted, and Slocum walked back to study their tracks. Not much to see. Probably only an Apache could trail them, he told the general.

But neither of them had any idea where they were.

They decided to spend the night in a friendly copse, and rolled in their blankets. In the morning they discovered they were nearly on the edge of the woods, and stretching north of them were grassy hills and clouds.

In the middle of the morning they halted under tall elms to wait out a light rain. When they went on they came to a fieldstone house on a rounded hill with a stone-cased well beside it and a corral behind that, with six mules staring at them.

As they came close they saw the sign: "Trading post L. Tanner Prop. Leve yur guns outside."

L. Tanner was Lucas Tanner, a big burly man with square white teeth and whiskers. He was glad to see them. "You's prob'ly the last I goin' to see till spring."

Tanner was living at the post with his young son, who was out hunting at the moment. His wife had been taken by the Lord a year ago, he told them. The whims of the Lord were damned peculiar.

He had really no more idea where he was than they did.

"I built this here post because it's on the north-south track of the Wichitas. I been tradin' with them nigh onto fifteen year."

"How far's the Mississippi, do you know?"

"Probably a hunnerd mile, give or take. I ain't been there in years. I was born over in east Tennessee. Ain't been there for a spell neither. You bring a newspaper with you?"

They had not. Tanner had not seen one for a very long time. He was proud that he could read, and was teaching his boy. It was drizzling outside when the boy returned, a big lanky shy lad with a rifle as tall as he. He'd had no luck and would try the next day.

Tanner let them sleep on the puncheon floor of the post that night after serving them some homemade whiskey.

"You drink enough of it," he promised, "and the mosquitoes won't bite you."

It tasted abominably. They learned its ingredients: a chunk of chewing tobacco, a handful of red pepper, a bottle of Jamaica ginger, a quart of molasses, and a dash of red ink all mixed up together with branch water. Now and then, Tanner said, he added a bit of kerosene for flavor.

The Indians bought it gleefully and thumped his counter for more.

It drizzled the next morning, and Tanner opened the heavy door to look out. "I 'spect my tradin's near done this year. Them Injuns'll be settin' in their lodges by the fire till grass-up."

McRae said, "And I expect you'll be doing the same."

"Guess so." Tanner grinned.

When the burly man and his son had gone to their beds in the back, McRae asked, "What does a man like Tanner do with the money he takes in?"

"He probably barters most things. But I imagine he buries his hard money somewhere."

"Yes. I suppose so. There're no banks within a week's journey, if that."

Slocum laughed. "He wouldn't trust a bank anyhow."

The general shrugged. "He's losing interest on his savings."

"I'll bet he doesn't even know what interest on money is."

"Is that possible?"

Slocum smiled. "You live in a different world, General. But Tanner is a man who could not live in a settled community. He would never fit in. He's part wolf, part hermit, and part pig iron. And he'll never change. And probably that boy of his will be exactly the same way."

McRae shook his head. "The country needs schools..."

"It needs a lot of things. But they come slowly to the people out in the sticks. Shall we hit the hay?"

"Let's do."

Buford Stark and Charlie turned inland from the great river after studying a map. Stark drew a line on the map, projecting the probable drift of the balloon. It would more than likely come down somewhere along that line—unless high winds blew it off course. How far would it drift? And when it came down, where would the two men go? Would they head south again?

Or return to the river?

Trying to put himself in the general's position and mind, Stark considered. *He*, in that case, would probably head for the river. After all, it was by far the quickest way south.

He discussed it with Charlie. And Charlie agreed with him.

So, since he and Charlie had investigated all the nearby river towns, the chances were good that the general and Slocum had not yet reached the river. They could be still on the way.

Stark drew more lines on the map. A huge, cone-shaped area. He tapped it with a pencil. "They're somewhere within those lines," he told Charlie.

Charlie shook his dark head. "That there's too big an area for two men t' search. It'd take a goddam regiment."

"But look at it again," Stark said. "There aren't that many towns. Damn few, in fact. It might not be such a big job when we get down to it."

"They might not be in a town."

Stark said sarcastically, "If they go through a town or stay in it overnight, people will notice. There's always porch-sitters. People look at strangers."

Charlie had to admit the logic of this.

Stark sent another wire and received the answer that nothing further had been forthcoming from the general. There could be any number of reasons why not.

The sender did not seem happy that so much time was being consumed, just to find two men.

"They got no idea what the hell we're up against," Stark told Charlie.

15

They started with the closest towns. Stark checked them off on the map. In the first three they had no luck. No one remembered two men of that description traveling together.

But in Yaleburg they struck pay dirt.

A hotel clerk said, "Yeah, they was two in here like that. They left maybe a week ago. Big ruckus about it, too."

"Why was that?"

"Because one of 'em broke the other out'n jail."

"What was he in jail for?"

"I ain't sure. I think the marshal said he was somebody on a poster. Wanted man."

"Is it possible the marshal made a mistake?"

The clerk shrugged. "Sure. Wouldn't be the first time. You want rooms?"

It was dark out, so they registered, and when they put their horses in the stable and went upstairs, the clerk sent a boy to tell the marshal that a man asking about the breakout was in the hotel saying he was the nephew of the escaped man.

Marshal Eddins came to call on Stark. He rapped on the door, and when Stark opened it, Eddins said, "Your uncle was through here a while back?"

"That's what the clerk tells me, yes."

The marshal pointed his pistol. "Get your coat. You're comin' with me."

"What?"

"You heard what I said."

Despite Stark's protestations, Eddins marched him to the jail and put him in a cell. "You'n your uncle is part of a gang and you ain't doin' this town while I'm marshal."

"But dammit! I'm not his nephew!"

"Oh? You're a liar, too, huh? Well, you shut your mouth or you gits nothin' to eat. Hear?"

The marshal left him in the dark.

Charlie Bannon learned that Stark was in jail when he rapped on Stark's door, then went down to ask the clerk if Stark had gone out.

"The marshal took him to the pokey."

"Why? What for?"

"He didn't tell me why."

Charlie went out to the stable and thought about it. Did the marshal have information that even Stark did not know? Maybe Stark had been arrested for an old crime. That was very likely, he thought. And if he, Charlie, went to the jail asking questions, he might also be implicated and tossed in a cell.

He did not wait any longer. He saddled his horse and rode out quietly, heading for the river. He would go upstream to St. Louis and find something else to do.

Let Stark take care of himself.

Stark was more frustrated than he had ever been. He had been arrested many times, but never for something he did not do. He knew from the hotel clerk that the marshal was in a fuming snit about the jailbreak. That of course was none of his doing, but he was somehow being blamed for it!

The damned hick marshal would not listen to reason. He had made up his stupid mind and would not change.

He should not have used the "uncle" dodge. But how was he to know?

And worst of all, there was no one to whom he could appeal. Eddins was the law in town. If there was a mayor, he did not know who . . . nor could he reach him if he knew. He was in jail, and he might as well have been in the middle of an ocean as far as talking to anyone.

When the deputy, Jed, brought him the skimpy pan of cold beans and chunk of hard bread, he would not say a word. He shook his head at all questions and got out, slamming the office door.

At first, Stark had hopes that Charlie would help. But Charlie did not come to the jail to argue his case. After the second day behind bars, Stark knew that Charlie had skedaddled. Charlie was a no-good and would not risk his own hide. Kiss him good-bye.

How to get out of the damned jail?

His best chance, he thought, was probably the deputy, Jed. A husky-enough looking young man, Jed was obviously not the smartest. He wore a pistol while shoving the food plate under the bars. If he could reach that pistol . . .

But each time he sidled close, Jed backed away.

Frustration made him raging angry. He slammed the chair in the cell, breaking it into splinters, tossing them through the bars, shouting. His shouts brought no one. Possibly they were used to it.

There was a thin mattress on the iron cot, and he pulled it apart, shoving it through the bars. He struck a match and set it afire. It took a while to get going; he blew on it and it flamed finally, with enormous amounts of smoke.

The white smoke filled the big room and drifted into the office.

Stark grinned evilly, hearing sudden shouts. Suddenly the office door slammed open and the portly marshal strode in, fanning smoke from his red face.

"What the goddam hell you doin', you crazy sonofabitch!" He stomped on the mattress, merely scattering it farther. He was coughing with the smoke and furious.

Stark threw pieces of the splintered chair at him, and the marshal poked at him through the bars in his fury. Stark grabbed an arm and heaved with all his strength. The marshal's head connected with a steel bar and he slumped, sprawling on the floor.

Stark glanced at the open office door. Was Jed out somewhere? He quickly shoved the marshal's gun in his belt and tore at the key ring on the other's belt. He opened the door on the third try, dragged the marshal inside, and locked the cell.

As he ran into the office, Jed came inside from the street. Jed stared at him openmouthed, and Stark shot him twice in the chest. Jed fell over a desk and slid bonelessly to the floor, dead.

Stark took his pistol and walked out into the evening air, closing the door behind him. Jed's horse was at the hitch rack. Smiling, he climbed aboard and rode out of town.

Slocum and the general discussed the lay of the land with Tanner, who had hunted over most of it. There were no towns close by, none between his store and the great river.

"Why don't y'all lay up here for a spell and rest? Me'n the boy is glad of the company."

It was a temptation. It would probably rain before they reached the river, Tanner said, and they'd be soaked. And the icy wind would cut into them . . . McRae said nothing at all, letting Slocum make the decision, but Slocum was sure he relished the idea of more rest.

Slocum said finally, "I don't see why we can't stay a bit longer—if you have room for us."

"Plenty room," Tanner said jovially. "Hell, iffen you'd stay the winter we could rig up some bunks in the back."

The boy's name was Boyd. He had just turned fifteen and was, his father claimed, as good a hunter and fisherman as any in the country. He had also learned tracking from Indian friends and could follow a duck's path through the air, Tanner said positively, a half hour after the duck had passed by.

Boyd owned a long cap-and-ball Kentucky rifle and was up and out of the post at dawn. He would do a bit of hunting, his father told them, and also see if anyone followed them.

It was a misty day, turning cold. There had been a neighbor family, Tanner told them, living only ten or twelve miles north, and they had visited often. The family had two girls, one thirteen that Boyd made goggle eyes at. But they had up and moved off, not able to make ends meet. It had been a sad day in Boyd's life.

Boyd appeared in several hours. He came in silently, startling McRae by his sudden presence, but his father was apparently used to having the boy materialize.

"What is it?"

"Stranger," Boyd said. " 'Bout a mile north, comin' along the trail. He be here in ten minutes."

"One man?"

Boyd nodded.

"What's he look like?"

"Buckskins, sorrel horse, Sharps rifle. Downwind drifter I'd say, lookin' to get somethin' easy."

He went out the back door, and Tanner stood in the front with his pipe. "Boyd didn't care for him much. He might be trouble."

He might be the sharp-nosed man, Slocum thought, except for the buckskins. He asked the general to go into the back room until they looked the stranger over.

The boy's guess seemed to be on the money. The stranger did look like a drifter. He came to the foot of the gentle hill and stared at the post.

Tanner puffed smoke. "Think he's a damn bounty hunter. Haven't seed one of 'em for a spell. He ought to be over by the river."

The man rode up to the door slowly and got down with a nod to Tanner. He was lean and weathered, with a four-day beard. He wore buckskins and a shapeless hat. There were two Navy pistols in his belt and a Sharps in the saddle scabbard on the horse. His black brows met in a single bushy line over his hooked nose, and he had a deep scar on his forehead.

"You ain't lost, are ye?" Tanner asked.

The man shook his head. "Heard you had a place here. So I come by. Can a man buy hisself a drink?"

"Come on in."

Tanner went behind the counter and took down a bottle of his special rotgut. "First drink's on the house." He poured into a dusty tumbler and pushed it across to the other.

The stranger looked at it against the light. "You Tanner?"

"Yep. That's me."

"M' name's Gillis. Here's yore health, Mr. Tanner." He gulped down the drink and made a terrible face.

Tanner grinned. "Ain't that good stuff?"

Gillis bared yellow teeth. "It tastes like boiled frogs. What the hell you put into it?" He wiped his mouth on a sleeve.

"Injuns likes it," Tanner said. He put the bottle back on the shelf.

Gillis turned to Slocum. "You live hereabouts, too?"

"Just passing through, Mr. Gillis. Like you are."

Gillis nodded. "Happens I looking for two men might come thisaway."

Tanner grunted. "You a bounty hunter?"

"I do a little of that now'n then, t'make ends meet. You seen two men travelin' together, Mr. Tanner?"

"You figger they come this way?"

"I was told that they might. What you say?"

Tanner shrugged. "That's hard to say. This here's a store and lots of folks come in. Was they any special scars or things on these here two men?"

"Names is McRae and Slocum. One's older'n the other."

"I see." Tanner scratched his belly. "I don't recollect any like that. What they wanted for?"

"Murder."

"Murder!" Slocum said in astonishment. "Who got murdered?"

"A deputy over to Yaleburg. Shot twice in the ticker. They was a jailbreak. It's on all the wires."

"I be damned," Tanner said. "I r'member that jail. Little slapped-together caboose with a fat marshal sittin' in it like a hen on 'er eggs. You care for 'nother drink, Mr. Gillis?"

"Think I'll pass." Gillis went to the door and looked at the sky. "I figger to git on to the river." He nodded to them and got on the sorrel horse.

Slocum watched him ride into the trees, heading west.

Behind him Tanner said, "Somebody shot a deputy?"

"I swear, it wasn't us." Slocum shook his head.

McRae came from the back room. "I heard what he said. Do you suppose it's true that someone shot the deputy?"

"It's prob'ly true," Tanner said, "or he wouldn't be here. His kind works on sure bets. Let's see what Boyd says when he comes in."

The boy did not appear until dark. Then he was suddenly with them, like a wraith.

Tanner asked, "Is he still out there?"

Boyd grinned. "He got him a camp 'bout a half mile over east. Right now he's a-settin' acrost the stream watchin' our door."

Slocum said, "He suspects us."

Boyd agreed. "He seen your hosses in the corral."

"It's only suspicion," McRae said softly. "How long do you think he'll wait there?"

Tanner shrugged. "Depends on how much he goin' to be paid. If they's a good bounty on you he'll stay there for a week—maybe more."

McRae looked at Slocum. "We shot no one, John. What do you figure this is about?"

"I can't guess, General. It may be a frame-up of some kind." Slocum sighed deeply. "What worries me is the telegraph. If they've put it out everywhere that we're guilty of murder . . ." He shook his head sadly.

Tanner said, "Usually it's dead or alive."

16

What did Gillis have in mind? Tanner advised them to stay inside. A rifle would reach them easily from across the stream. Slocum thought the man would wait until they left and follow, hoping to get the drop.

Boyd said, "It'd be easy to fix 'is wagon. You want me to—"

"No." Slocum said thanks. He did not want anyone shot from ambush.

Tanner said, "Just keep a watch on 'im. Let us know what he does."

Boyd nodded and went out the rear door.

McRae said, "What if Gillis sees the boy? He might do him harm."

Tanner laughed. "He ain't goin' to get a sight of that lad. Don't you worry none. Boyd, he knows ever' blade of grass and ever' rock for fifty mile around. Even if he *did* see him, Gillis would never catch 'im. If they was hurt in the picture, you ought to worry about Gillis."

Boyd returned after dark to report that Gillis had gone to his camp and made a fire. Apparently he did not expect them to leave the post at night.

"So that's what we'll do," Slocum said. "Let's get our fixings together."

"Where you pointin' for?"

Slocum glanced at the general. "Probably to the river."

McRae nodded.

They saddled the horses long after dark, settled up with their host, and said good-byes. Boyd led them away from the post along a trail that neither of them could see in the gloom. He led them through twists and turns to a road of sorts and left them, lifting a hand in farewell. Slocum saw a sheen of white teeth, then the boy was gone like a shadow in the night.

"I'd hate to have *him* after me," McRae said in a heartfelt tone.

They followed the road westward, moving at a walk along the edge of it. Wagons had churned deep ruts that were dry and hard on hoofs. The track wound through the dark trees that sometimes met overhead in intricate tracings, often hiding the thin crescent of icy moon.

They had gone only a few miles when the sun came hesitantly over the far hills. Slocum thought the bounty hunter would notice their horses were not in the corral, and he would then look for tracks. How good a tracker was he?

In the morning they halted off the trail to rest. The general was tired and dropped off to sleep. Slocum let him nap for several hours longer than he had intended.

A farm wagon, driven by an older man with a boy on the seat beside him, came along in the middle of the morning, heading west. Soon after, three men on mules came from the direction of the river, with several dogs running along with them. When they disappeared it was very still. Slocum watched a pair of hawks swooping and diving far off over the trees. If they saw no evidence of the sharp-nosed man or the bounty hunter, they might well get passage on a boat and go downstream. Perhaps outrun them both. After all, it was not possible to watch every inch of the river . . .

He woke the general, and they looked to the cinches and prepared to go on. Mounting, they rode out to the road, and as they turned into it, the shots came.

The general was hit by the first shot!

He fell from the horse, and Slocum instantly threw himself off and lay in the grass, the Colt firing almost before he hit the ground. The shots came from brush on the far side of the road, and he fired at the source of the smoke two, three, four, five times.

Suddenly it was quiet. Slocum crawled to McRae, who was huddled in the tall grass, holding his upper arm, which was bloody. Slocum made a quick inspection; the blood was not pumping out, so an artery had not been hit. He could not determine whether the bone was broken. He did his best to stop the bleeding, wrapping McRae's torn shirt about it. Gritting his teeth, McRae asked how bad it was.

"I can't tell. Can you hold the arm tightly . . . Yes, like that." Slocum reloaded the revolver.

"Are you going after him?"

"I have to, or we'll be pinned down here, and we've got to get you back to Tanner's place."

McRae nodded mutely.

Keeping a close watch on the spot where the shots had come from, Slocum crawled away. Their two horses had run a short distance and were now cropping grass. He crawled to the road. Was the sniper the bounty hunter? Probably.

Slocum lay quiet for several moments, studying the brush and trees. Gillis had undoubtedly moved since his first shots. He could be anywhere, right or left. The first spot was about twenty yards from the road across a grassy expanse.

He looked back and could barely see the general's shape in the grass, unmoving. Gillis might think him dead.

Slocum was in tall weeds at the edge of the road, in good cover. But he had to cross the road to get at Gillis. It had to be done. If he tried to put the general on a horse, Gillis could easily shoot them both down. The only way to save McRae was to get Gillis.

He took a deep breath, then, gathering himself, he jumped up and sprinted across the road. No shots came. He dropped into the grass and rolled. Still no shots.

He ran again, the Colt extended, hammer back. It took forever to gain the brush. Halting, he listened, hearing only distant birds. Cautiously he moved to the spot where the shots had come from—and found blots of dark blood on the leaves. He had hit the sniper!

The trail was easy to follow. Gillis had lost a considerable amount of blood. He would probably go to his horse . . .

Slocum ducked low, hearing what sounded like someone mounting a horse close by. Picking up a rock, he tossed it to his left. As it rattled in the brush, Gillis fired. Slocum hurried forward. The bounty hunter was on the sorrel horse, leaning far over the pommel, trying to control the horse, which danced in a tiny clearing.

Gillis saw him then. His eyes widened and he raised the revolver. Both men fired, and Gillis's shot went into the air. He was knocked from the saddle—dead when he hit the ground.

There was nothing on the body but matches and tobacco, a few coins, and a sheath knife. He put them in the saddlebags on the sorrel with Gillis's two Navy Colts. He mounted the horse and rode back to the general.

McRae was in pain. "I—I heard shots . . ."

"It was Gillis who followed us. He's back there in the weeds." He looked at the wound again. The bleeding had stopped. "We've got to get you back to Tanner's. It's the closest place by miles." The wound was on the outside of the arm, which was good. The big artery was on the inside. If the bullet had hit that, the general would probably be gone.

There was nothing more he could do. "You've got to ride, General. Are you up to it?"

"I'll have to be . . ."

Slocum helped him to his feet, and he swayed and leaned heavily. "Maybe I could rest a little longer . . . ?"

"No. You're stronger now than you will be later. We've got to put you in a bed before the fever starts."

"I didn't think it would happen to me . . ."

"Let's get you on the horse."

McRae held the horn with his left hand, and Slocum boosted him up. McRae got a leg over and hunched in the saddle. Slocum put both feet in the stirrups.

"Now, hang on, General."

Slocum mounted and held the sorrel's reins. They began to move at a walk. He rode close beside the other and reached out now and then, but McRae clenched his teeth and, though the pain must be considerable, Slocum knew, he did not make a whimper.

It was important to keep him conscious. If McRae lapsed into unconsciousness he would undoubtedly slide off the horse, reopening the wound and causing other complications.

Slocum kept up a busy conversation, forcing the general to reply, "What was that?" or "What did you say?" Insisting on answers, he said outrageous things, so much so that McRae often stared at him in astonishment. He told all the jokes and stories he knew, talked about people he had known, insisting that McRae give opinions, and when the wounded man fell into silence, Slocum shook him, saying, "Wake up, stay awake . . ." He questioned him about the war, pulling answers out of him, and the miles plodded by.

He had not seen a wagon at Tanner's store, else he would have left the general and ridden to bring it back. They did not meet anyone along the road.

After several hours, he began to worry about the turnoff. How would he know when to move off the road? The path they had followed from the trading post would probably be apparent only to someone like Boyd, who was part of the woods. If they followed a wrong path they might never find the trading post at all.

He recalled then what an old-timer had once told him. In the days before roads, a man could get lost while approaching a habitation he was unfamiliar with. So he would fire his gun at intervals into the air, till someone came out to find *him*.

When he approached the area where he thought they might have come onto the road, he warned the general, then fired his pistol into the air at five-minute intervals.

He grinned when he saw Boyd ride toward him, the long Kentucky across his thighs.

Boyd was not at all surprised they had met up with Gillis. He recognized the sorrel horse instantly and led them through the woods to the post.

Burly Tanner came running out, lifted the general bodily from the horse, and carried him inside to lay him on a cot.

"Did Gillis shoot him?"

Slocum nodded, leaning over the older man. The general's eyes were closed, his face drawn with pain. It was obvious he was exhausted.

Tanner examined the bandaged wound and shook his head. There was nothing more he could do. In the store he said, "It's up to him now. He either goin' to make it or he don't."

"Where's the nearest doctor?"

"I don't even know. Maybe a hunnerd mile." Tanner shook his dark head. "He got to smart it out. You sure it was Gillis, hah?"

"That's his horse outside. Boyd saw him on it."

"You plug 'im?"

"Had to. Had to leave the body in the woods. Nothing else to do. You might as well have the horse. And there's two pistols in the saddlebags."

Tanner smiled. "We'll give the horse to Boyd. That nag he ridin' is gettin' on. And Gillis, he ain't likely to be a gent had many friends who'd come a-lookin' for him."

"I doubt very much if his mother liked him."

Tanner laughed. "That calls for a drink."

Slocum made a face. "Not your rotgut!"

"Oh, that's for Injuns. I got real whiskey, too." He brought a bottle from under the counter and poured into two glasses. "I bet they ain't a Injun west o' St. Louis ever in his life had a drink of real good whiskey."

"Too bad, but that'll change."

Tanner sighed. "Ever'thing changes."

17

Stark rode to the next town he had marked on his map. It was Roselle, not more than a wide place in the road, and he learned nothing except that the general had not been there.

The next town was on the telegraph. When he saw the poles he waited till dark before riding in. He might be a wanted man by now. But he saw no posters, and he asked few questions, not wishing to draw attention to himself. Neither the general nor Slocum sat in either of the saloons. The four-room hotel, hardly worthy of the name, did not shelter them either.

He sent a wire in the morning and waited impatiently for the reply. But it was a disappointment. Nothing had been heard from the general. He might have dropped into a hole too deep to climb out of.

Stark left the town and headed toward the west, making a wide swing around Yaleburg. It took him nearly a week to ride back to the Mississippi. And when he saw it flowing majestically past, it made him feel a deep gloom.

Where would he go now?

Was the general upriver, or down? Or near the river at all? It had lured him, like a siren to a sailor on the deep, and now it was taunting him. He could almost see it smile, and he turned his back.

He rode south till he came to a little river town, not on the telegraph, and put up at the local hostelry. No one he talked to had seen a man of the general's description.

Tanner had a few patent medicines on the shelf but nothing that would help the general, and he suffered. A fever gripped him and held him in its sweaty hands. Slocum sat by him for hours, putting cold pads of cloth on his forehead, easing him as much as possible. Tanner hovered by them, wanting to help, but there was nothing he could do.

When it rained heavily outside, Boyd came in, restless as a cougar. The instant the rain let up he was out into the woods with his long rifle. He brought back rabbits and a small deer. He made a wide circle around the trading post and found no other human tracks. He made the circle every day when it was clear. The tracks of animals were everywhere, he told Slocum, but the post was not being watched by human eyes.

That, at least, was comforting.

Weeks passed before the general's fever broke, and when it did, he was weak as a kitten . . . but able to smile again. Slocum fed him soup and meat broth and a bit of bread, a little more each day; he had lost too much weight.

It snowed constantly as Christmas approached. Tanner had a big black iron stove in the middle of the post store that kept both rooms warm. He and Boyd had chopped enough wood during the summer to keep Kansas City warm, he said. It was ricked up at the back of the building under a slanting roof.

He also had a huge supply of airtights—they were delivered to him in a wagon each spring—and Boyd kept them in meat. "There ain't nothing we need," Tanner said, "but a woman or two."

The end of December came and went. McRae sat by the big stove each day, gradually getting his strength back. His right arm had a terrible scar; he was sure the bone had been nicked, but he was lucky it had not been broken. A man on a horse is in constant movement, and Gillis's bullet had certainly been aimed at his heart. But the motion of the horse had put it through the upper arm instead, a matter of a few inches.

Gillis had doubtless intended to shoot both of them. But Slocum's action, throwing himself off the horse instantly, had made that impossible. And Slocum's accuracy, firing at the powder smoke of Gillis's gun muzzle, had done the sniper in. Gillis's mistake, as the general mentioned to Tanner, was to shoot at him first instead of Slocum.

It was a mild winter, according to both Boyd and his father, but the snow piled deep. The stream was frozen, and Boyd had to chop holes in it to fish. He fashioned a new pair of snowshoes each summer; he went hunting every week to keep them in meat. Now and then Slocum went with him for the exercise, though he was sure he slowed the boy up.

As the weeks sped by the general recovered rapidly. Once the healing had begun he swore he felt better each day. He played checkers with Tanner, talked about the late war, and began to get restless. He put back the weight he'd lost, and when spring melted the ice and snow, and brown water filled the creeks and streams, he was ready to go.

He was sure their enemies had given up the chase.

Slocum did not agree.

Buford Stark considered going back upriver to St. Louis for the winter . . . until he rode into Pannis, on the river, and saw the poster: WANTED FOR MURDER. It had a good description of himself, and his name. He was worth five hundred dollars dead or alive for killing a deputy marshal.

He rode out again quickly.

He dared not go on to St. Louis after seeing that. The posters were probably spread up and down the river. He knew a number of people in St. Louis, and any one of them, he was sure, would love to turn him in for less than five hundred.

He was very low on funds and wired to get more, saying he was on the general's tail. The reply asked him for details and he made up some that sounded good. He was told to see Mr. Ricard, manager of the Farnham Bank.

Farnham was fifty miles inland, west of the river, and it took him nearly four days to get there, partway in the rain, a miserable ride. He arrived out of sorts and bedraggled, but the hotel had a room, and a hot meal and dry clothes helped his disposition. He had ruined his coat in the rain; it had turned pulpy and became so shapeless that he had to toss it away. He bought another at the dry goods store.

Mr. Ricard proved to be a rotund little man, fussy as a bureaucrat, with steel-rimmed glasses and shiny head. He had a wire authorizing him to make payment to Buford Stark and insisted on credentials.

Stark said, "How would I know about the draft if I weren't the right person? I wired to ask for it."

Ricard had to admit there was a certain logic in that argument and finally allowed the money to be paid.

Farnham was not a small town. It was on the Cedar River and enjoyed a bustling river traffic. It fed into the Mississippi. Stark looked for and saw no posters at all in the town. His hotel, the Cedar House, adjoined the Palace Saloon, which in its turn encompassed an upstairs bordello.

His first evening in town, Stark met Cora. She was a shapely cyprian who worked out of an upstairs bed, dividing her time between exercises on the bed and luring glances in the saloon. Stark's new coat impressed her; he was easily the best-dressed man in the noisy room. So she hung on to his arm, rubbing herself against him—she had plenty to rub. It was a tactic Stark enjoyed and finally succumbed to.

They went upstairs and spent an hour in her bed, doing somewhat the same dance the girls did on the small stage in the saloon, except they did it horizontally.

Cora was sure he had money. In the bed she felt his money belt, and it thrilled her. Money did more for her than love. Many of her customers had to save up for a visit with her, so she clung to him even after they went downstairs again.

As a rule she paid as little attention as possible to a client, certainly in the matter of looks, because most of them were weather-beaten or bushy faced, and many were downright ugly, with breath that would curl an iron bar. Stark was not handsome; in other circumstances she would not have given him a second glance. She cared little for people who had squinty eyes and sharp noses. But the feel of that belt . . .

Stark—he told her his name was Fred—had money in his kick, and most did not. She never asked him where he got it nor did she care. As long as she got some of it. And to do that, she made him think he was something very special—which he was willing to believe.

Cora did not live in the upstairs cubicle, of course. That was only her workplace. She had a room in Mrs. Wallis's boardinghouse and slept half the morning each day, depending on how long the night had been. Mrs. Wallis catered to girls like Cora, since she had been one of them herself years ago, before she had married one of her customers and settled into a life of semi-respectability. She was not completely respectable because of her boarders, and because she drank a good portion of a bottle of whiskey a day. To Mrs. Wallis the world always had a kind of rosy aura about it.

When she was sober, not often, she was impossible. She swore like a mule skinner and threw things—anything at hand—on the least provocation.

The third night Stark went upstairs with Cora, she had a suggestion. Why didn't he move out of the hotel and come to stay with her?

It was an interesting proposition, and Stark considered it. The posters were likely to appear at any time, and winter was close, which would make travel inconvenient. Also Cora was exciting as hell in bed. She knew tricks he hadn't yet thought of. And she was genuinely fond of him. Why else would she want him to be close all the time?

On her part, Cora was sure she would be better able to get at his money belt, perhaps when he was asleep. And if there was enough cash, she would then perform the Dance of the Seventh Veil . . . to wit: Disappear. Into thin air. Good-bye.

She had performed this gyration several times before, and once the money she had tucked into her traveling bag had kept her all year long. She had not had to resort even once to the supine position. She had great hopes for Fred's belt. She had in fact a gambler friend/lover who would take her in and hide her during the time Fred raged and searched for her after he discovered his loss.

Cora was a girl who thought ahead.

When Stark saw Mrs. Wallis's boardinghouse and realized all the tenants were girls of Cora's stripe, he assented at once. He would be the only male in a house full of soiled doves! His ship had come in!

Cora was right enough in her assumption. Stark did have a considerable amount of money. He had changed most of it into gold eagles and shoved all of them into a leather money belt, which he wore about his middle at all times, except when he was in bed with her. Then he usually took it off with the rest of his clothes. But before he went to sleep he put it on again. It would be impossible for anyone to undo the buckle without waking him.

It was a problem she had not foreseen and could not overcome . . . outside of stabbing him. And she seriously considered it. She discussed the situation with her gambler friend; his name was Rufe Brull, a tall, skinny man, pasty faced and long fingered. He had the morals of a wheelbarrow and was somewhat in favor of the stabbing, but he worried that the law in Farnham was fairly competent.

He said, "You'd have to kill him in Mrs. Wallis's house. Otherwise he'd be discovered too soon."

"I changed my mind. I d'want to stab him."

"Why not?"

"I might mess it up. If I didn't do it right the first second, he'd be up and he'd kill me."

Brull nodded, frowning. There was that. But shooting would be too noisy. It would wake the house. He studied her, wondering if she could take an axe to him. He sighed. Maybe not. She was not very strong, never having done a day's work in her life. She had chosen a career where her customers did all the work. She merely provided the orifice.

She was staring at him, and he knew at once what she was thinking. She wanted him to do it. Her thinking ran that way—let the man do it.

He put her off, saying he would like to take a good look at Fred first. Was he a gunman? She didn't know. Was he a holdup man? Where did he get his money?

She said the same to all. "I dunno. But he's got it. His money belt is heavy as hell. He's got gold in it."

Brull stared at Fred as he sat in the saloon at a table with several others, playing a quiet game of poker. He looked sly, Brull thought, and he might be rattler quick with a gun. It was hard as hell to judge a man's fighting abilities just by gazing at him. He had once seen a squat little fat man haul out an iron and shoot up a saloon, killing three men, just because he got mad about something. You never could tell.

He watched Fred most of the evening, and it was easy to see he packed a gun under his coat. Not all men carried weapons, but the ones who did usually could use them. He concluded Fred might be a very dangerous customer.

When he talked again with Cora he said, "Shooting's the only way. He'll have to be surprised with a gun at close range. I wouldn't trust a knife."

"I could let you in the house when he's asleep . . ."

"No . . . that's out. One of the girls might see me. They're up at all hours, and they'd turn me in for a half dime. No. It's gotta be done outside."

"He doesn't go outside much. Just to the saloon and back."

"Hmm. Well, that's a couple hunnerd yards. I'll look at it tomorrow."

The back door of the saloon was on an alley where the line of privies stood, doors standing open. Above them was a lantern on a wire; the lamp could be moved back and forth to light the privy someone wanted to use.

To get to Mrs. Wallis's boardinghouse it was necessary to cross the wide alley and walk between two houses and around a corner. It was very dark between the houses at night, and the sound of a shot might be muffled somewhat.

Brull walked back and forth a few times. He would have to shoot Fred between the houses, then get the money belt off him in the pitch dark—that would take a few minutes. If someone heard the shot and investigated, how long would it take them to get there? The timing might be tricky, but on the other hand, the someone might not be in a hurry to enter the dark area. He'd go for a lantern first.

It had been raining off and on, as they planned their move. And then one night it began snowing. It snowed all the next day, in all about two feet.

When he looked out at the white expanse, Brull smiled. Maybe snow was the answer! He would shoot Fred, then cover the body with snow—and it might not be discovered till spring. Everyone would assume Fred had moved on, if they thought about him at all. If they asked Cora, she would say Fred had told her he was going.

Then he and Cora would be free to leave, not in haste, but before spring. When the body was uncovered, they would be a very long way off. They would also change their names. Even if they were accused, no one could prove anything.

Now they would wait for the next snowstorm.

18

Their preparations to leave were simple: saddle the horses, tie on the food sacks, and say their good-byes. The general declared himself ready for anything.

The two of them had formed a considerable attachment for the big burly Lucas Tanner and his woodsman son, and they swore they would return one day. Boyd accompanied them out to the road and a few miles along it, assuring them once more that no one had watched the trading post. No one knew where they were. He waved one last time and disappeared into the woods.

"Now we face reality again," the general said with a sigh. Boyd's daily rounds had been a great comfort. He felt as if they'd lost a good measure of protection.

But it was a lovely, brisk spring morning and enemies must be far off. None could possibly know where they'd wintered.

They found that Tanner had been right about the river. It was at least a hundred miles distant, and they were a week along the road, struggling across swollen streams and churning sometimes through ankle-deep mud. They met very few travelers and saw very few signs of habitation.

It was a sparsely settled region.

The murky Mississippi was a welcome sight, even though they saw it through a light spring rain, in the shelter of a pine woods. They had obviously reached the great river at the beginning of one of its vast loops, and they elected to go across the bight and meet it again farther south.

When they did, they came to the little town of Brewer. One of the first things they noticed on riding in was a poster tacked to the front of the livery. WANTED FOR MURDER! It described the sharp-nosed man and named him: Buford Stark. He was wanted for the murder of a deputy marshal.

So that was his name!

The poster was another welcome sight. It meant their chief enemy would of necessity be somewhat curtailed in his movements. Five hundred dollars was a fortune to most, and people would be looking hard at strangers.

The town boasted no hotel, but the saloon owner, Enos Hook, rented out cubicles on the second floor above the bar. The cells had been once occupied by floozies, he told them, plying their trade. But the town had gone heavy Baptist in the last few years and he'd had to shoo them out. He sighed as he said this.

It had been a long time since Slocum had made a report to Reardon and Munch. He discussed it with the general, who felt that a report should be made, even though there was a danger that the wire would be read by the wrong person.

He asked, "Is there any way we can protect ourselves from it?"

Slocum shrugged. "We can send the wire, then move from here quickly."

"Then let's do it that way. Besides, this Stark person must be in hiding, and he may be hundreds of miles from us. It would be an enormous coincidence if he were anywhere near."

Slocum agreed. He composed the message and had it sent off. They had survived the winter and were both well. McRae was in good spirits.

He did not mention the shooting and McRae's recovery. That was all in the past. He did say, "Someone is reading the wires. Make a change."

A telegram was sent to Stark in Farnham. The general had surfaced in the little town of Brewer on the river. It suggested Stark go there at once.

It was not a request.

Stark bought the necessities and decided not to tell Cora . . . knowing how whoregirls gossiped. He would simply go, and come back when the job was done. He would be free then, too. And with money. Free, except for the Wanted posters.

He played cards in the saloon as he always did, acting as ordinary as possible. He left the saloon at the usual time and started home to Mrs. Wallis's house. Cora was still upstairs plying her trade. She would get home late, too late to start asking questions about where he had gotten to. It would give him many hours' head start.

He did leave a note on her pillow saying he would be back.

When he left the saloon it was a misty night with no moon and very quiet. He crossed the alley and entered the dark space between the houses—and hesitated. He had traversed this path dozens of times before, but suddenly it seemed more than quiet. He had run from the law for years and had developed a sixth sense. And that, coupled with the posters, made him very alert.

He thought about the posters he had seen. He was worth five hundred dollars dead or alive. It was a lot of money to someone who had none. Had somebody in the town seen one and made the connection? It was quite possible.

He drew the pistol and, muffled by his coat, cocked it.

Edging into the narrow space, he moved a step at a time, listening, with the pistol out before him. Maybe he was just being overcautious . . .

Halfway along there was a brick chimney jutting out.

Was there movement behind it—a glimpse of metal? Stark was wearing a white shirt under the coat. He pulled the coat close and went to one knee, glancing back to see if he was silhouetted. He was not.

Silently he moved to the side, pressing himself tight against the house wall. If there *was* an assassin there, behind the chimney, he could not go forward. He'd best go back. A gunfight in a confined place could be fatal to one or both.

He began to move back.

And suddenly there was a blossom of orange flame, a thunderous report, and the bullet rapped into something far behind him. Instantly Stark fired back, once, twice, three times, then ran. He gained the alley before another shot came searching for him.

His horse was in Mrs. Wallis's stable and his blanket roll on Cora's bed. It took him a half hour to work his way around and enter the house from another direction. He heard no more from the assassin. He picked up the bedroll and moved silently to the stable, keeping the pistol ready.

Lighting a lamp, he saddled his horse, tied on the blankets and a food sack, and blew out the light. He opened the alley door gently and climbed on the horse. He walked the mount out slowly, only a shadow in the night.

Two shots greeted him, and he fired back instantly at the muzzle blast and dug in the spurs.

In less than ten minutes he was at the edge of town, loping along a dimly seen track. He reloaded the pistol, wondering who had shot at him.

Cora went home at midnight to find the note on the pillow. Fred had gone somewhere? She had heard shots earlier, but they were not uncommon in the town. Had Rufe Brull disposed of Fred? If he had, why was he not here in the room to greet her—and show her the money belt?

A lot of unanswered questions. She went to bed, a frown on her face.

She woke in the morning to the news that Brull's body had been discovered in the alley. He had a revolver in his hand and had been shot through the eye.

Fred's horse was gone from the stable. She could only assume that Fred had met Brull in the alley and Brull had lost. Fred's note said nothing about why he had gone . . . It was a mystery.

The local marshal questioned everyone he thought might know something. But no one had any idea why Rufe had been in the alley or who he had fought with.

He did not ask Cora. What would she know? He knew she had been seeing Brull. If she had not been a floozy he might think someone had trifled with her affections and Brull had protested, but any farmhand with a dollar could buy her affections.

Stark went directly to the river, consulting his map. The town of Brewer was north, hard to tell how far. The map was vague about distances. It took him four days to get there, and he arrived at night.

He quickly learned the saloon owner, Enos Hook, rented rooms on the second floor but had no tenants at the moment. The last two had gone several days before. No, Enos did not know where.

Stark had not seen them on the road, so they had not gone south—on this side of the river. But maybe they had crossed over. However, he could find no boatman who had taken them. He returned to the saloon and rented one of the cubicles for the night.

And when he went upstairs with his bedroll, Enos went out and down the street to the marshal's office.

"Hello, Joe. I want to collect five hunnerd."

"You do? What for?"

Enos pointed to one of the posters on the wall. "I got that feller in one o' my rooms right now."

"No joshin'?"

"It's the God's truth. He come in tonight. Told me his

name was Fred Smith. He'll be in bed asleep b' now."

"Them rooms got keys?"

"Hell no. Just turn-bars inside. Any one of them doors'll slam open if you shove 'em hard."

"You're sure it's him?"

"Positive. The description matches exact." Enos scratched his chin. "You goin' to sit there?"

The marshal got to his feet. "Cool down, Enos. We'll git him. You figger he's asleep, huh? I'll go by and get Frank."

Enos nodded and went to the door. "Don't shoot up the place, Joe. Tired of patchin' the roof."

19

Marshal Joe Pettus walked to the end of town and across a field to Frank Toms's shack and got him out of bed. Frank was his only deputy—on call when he was needed. Usually he worked three days a week. There was no crime in Brewer, only drunks.

He rattled the door. "Frank!"

"Who izzit?"

"It's me. Get your ass out. We got a job."

There was a pause. "At this time o' night, for crissakes?"

"Best time. The hombre's asleep. Come on. Shake loose."

Frank crawled out reluctantly and pulled on his pants and boots. He shoved the Starr into his belt, and they went back to the saloon. The suspect was still in his room, Enos told them. They went up the inside stairs.

At the room both men drew pistols. Joe listened at the flimsy door for a minute, nodding to Frank. He could hear the sound of steady breathing. In another cubicle someone was snoring.

With a look at Frank, the marshal stepped back, then lunged at the door with his shoulder. It crashed open, and

Buford Stark opened his eyes wide to stare into the muzzle of the marshal's gun.

"Git up, Mr. Stark. You under arrest."

Frank tied the prisoner's hands behind him, and they marched him down the street to the jail and gave him a cell all to himself.

Buford protested on the way. "You got the wrong man—my name's not Stark!"

"That's for a judge to decide, Mr. Stark. In the meantime you keep on lookin' like him."

"You got the wrong man!"

"You goin' back to Yaleburg, Mr. Stark, to stand trial. And I tell you, they goin' to hang your ass. You ought t'know better than to shoot a deppity."

Stark said, "I didn't shoot nobody!"

" 'Course not."

In the morning the marshal wired Yaleburg to say they had Stark in jail. He also said a citizen was claiming the five-hundred-dollar reward. Marshal Eddins wired back. He would send a man to fetch Stark. And the reward would be paid as soon as Stark was convicted. That should not take any time at all.

Marshal Pettus went home to his wife every night. He was appointed by his cronies, the town elders, and had a certain standing in the community, having been marshal for more than thirty years.

Frank Toms, on the other hand, was poor as a horned toad, had no schooling, and had never been able to hold a job. Pettus paid him slave wages for his part-time work and felt that Frank should be more grateful. Frank slept on a cot in the jail office when they had prisoners in the cells.

He had never been married and was not the brightest, but he usually obeyed orders and never asked why he had to do all the nasty jobs and was paid pennies. Frank had long since learned that he was one of the have-nothings. And so he expected nothing.

Buford Stark showed an interest in him the instant the marshal left the building. Frank was unused to anyone giving him a second look, even a prisoner, and he listened, his jaw slack, as Stark assured him the marshal was going off half cocked. "You got the wrong man, Mr. Toms."

Mr. Toms! He had never been called that in his life!

Stark had a handful of gold eagles and let them drop in a golden glitter from one hand to the other as he talked.

Frank stared at them in a kind of awe, never having seen so much money before. Real gold eagles!

"This's for you," Stark said softly. "Open the door and look the other way."

"The marshal would kill me!"

"No, the marshal will not kill you," Stark corrected. "You will walk out of here and take the next steamboat. You'll have enough money in your kick to buy anything you want. You could go to St. Louis!" Stark smiled winningly. "You'll be in some beautiful girl's arms while he's yelling. You can buy 'em pretty things, Frank. You'll have all the girls you want!" He showered the glittering coins from one hand to the other. "They'll be all over you, Frank, hugging you, kissing you—and other things. Have you any idea what you can do with money?"

"I—I never had none."

Stark jingled the coins under the other's nose. "There's three hundred dollars here, Frank. It's all yours. All I want is my horse and gun and a few hours' start."

Frank took deep breaths, staring at the gold. "He—he'll know I let you out."

"I told you," Stark said patiently. "You'll be on a steamboat headed away from here. He'll never touch you. There's steamboats come here at night, huh?"

"Oh yeah, sure."

"Well, he won't know where you've gone. You just won't be here in the morning. What's to hold you in this town?"

Frank shook his head slowly. "I—I got to think about it."

Stark showered the coins from one hand to the other again. "Think about this, Frank."

Slocum and the general rode north from Brewer. That was the direction least likely to be suspected. After a few miles they came to a flatboat, hailed it, and were taken across to the other shore with their horses.

If their wires were being read by the wrong people, Stark was sure to be notified they'd been in Brewer very recently. But with luck that was the last message an unauthorized person would see. Steps would certainly be taken to make the telegraphs more secure.

As they rode, Slocum thought seriously about going back to Brewer and confronting Stark if and when he arrived. But the general would have none of it, saying Stark might well have a half dozen men with him.

A fast-moving rainstorm drove them into the near woods. It was tolerably dry under the thick branches; they built a fire and spent the night feeding it.

The general's arm was healed, but still it was causing him considerable pain. "It's very like rheumatism," he said. "I expect it's the weather."

Warmth did not help particularly; the twinges did not go away even when he sat close to the hot fire. But the next day, when the sun came out, the arm felt better. The cold rain had passed, leaving the sky washed clean and the air crisp. They looked for a path or trail but found none, so the going was slow.

On the third day after crossing the river, Slocum's horse went lame. He got down at once, rubbed his hand along the shoulder of the animal and slid it down to the cannon bone. Lifting the hoof, he could see nothing wrong except the shoes were very worn.

He glanced at McRae. "Probably needs redoing. I'll walk a bit, see if that helps."

It did not. After a mile or more the horse still limped. The general squinted into the far haze. "I'll ride on there a few miles. Perhaps the next town's not far."

"All right."

It was a pleasant day for a walk. He watched the general's figure grow small in the distance. A breath of dust curled away from his path, then he was gone.

He was back inside the hour. "There is a town, maybe five miles. I could see it from a little bluff. How's the walking?"

"Could be worse."

The general swung down and walked with him. "At least it's not raining."

The town was "Runemede, pop 874," according to a sign alongside a rutted path. It was a tiny place on a brown meadow, but it had a blacksmith, who looked at the four shoes.

"They wore down to the nails," he said.

Slocum nodded. "I expect they need replating all round."

"Yep."

The smith removed the old shoes and brushed the hoofs deftly with a stiff brush. "The frogs is all right..." He pared the toes to receive the new shoes, and the pungent odor of dirty hoofs filled the small shop. Then he worked the bellows to the fire and prepared to heat the front shoes.

Slocum said, "You don't get many travelers here."

"Not many. You's the first I seen for a couple weeks come in on hosses. Most folks passes us by, even on the river." He smiled. "I guess we's just too damn small t'count."

"That's not good for business."

"Oh, I got plenty to keep me busy. Farm business like busted wagons, windmill blades, and wheels." He tapped the anvil. "Horseshoes like yours." He straightened up and laid his hammer aside. "Take 'im over there crost the road, and lemme have a look."

Slocum walked the horse across and back as the smith squatted and watched, squinting one eye. "That's fine. He walks all right now."

Slocum thanked the man and paid him. He joined the general, and they had a meal in the restaurant; it had two tables and two stools at a little counter. He said, "The blacksmith says he hasn't seen strangers in a while."

McRae nodded toward the woman busy behind the counter. "She told me the same."

As they paid the bill the general asked the woman, "What's the next town south?"

"Grafton. It's about forty mile."

When they went out to the horses, the general said, "Grafton! I'll be damned, Grafton!"

Slocum looked at him curiously. "What is it?"

"One of my staff in the war lived in Grafton. Colonel George Schmidt. I wonder if he is still there . . ."

"I'd say a good chance. And you would like to see him again?"

"I certainly would!"

There was a road leading south, and they rode all the rest of the day. If the town was forty miles away, it was a very long forty. Someone had guessed generously. They spent the night in a woods and did not arrive till nearly noon the next day.

They asked for Schmidt in a saloon and learned he lived not in the town but five or six miles outside it. The bartender came out to the street with them and pointed out the road to take.

The Schmidt house was on a slight rise of ground, surrounded by tall elms and a few pines. There was also a barn, several weathered sheds, and a corral. Chickens fluttered from their path as they rode in. Schmidt was on a corral pole as a rider was breaking a horse. He turned, hearing the horses, stared and yelped in astonishment, and nearly fell off the pole.

"Jesus Christ! It's General McRae!"

He got down and ran to the horse. "My God, General, it's good to see you! Where the hell did you fall from?"

"Hello, George." McRae got down and they embraced. "You haven't changed a bit!"

"Neither have you—well, you're a little pale."

McRae presented Slocum and they shook hands. Schmidt was a stout man, gray-haired and middle-aged, but he still looked spry and unwrinkled. He called someone to look after the horses and led them to the house.

His wife, Marna, came to greet them, delighted to see McRae after so many years. The general kissed her hand, saying she had not aged a minute since they had last met in Richmond.

She smiled. "That must be ten years ago . . ."

"The years are kinder to some of us than to others."

Schmidt came in with a bottle and poured into glasses, handing them around. He clinked glasses with McRae. "Well, General, we lost it, but I think people will remember that we tried hard."

McRae laughed. "That they will, George. It will be hard to put behind us."

"What are you doing in this part of the country? I thought you had returned to the law in San Francisco."

"Yes, I did. But I foolishly took my pen in hand and wrote my memoirs. It was the beginning of endless trouble. And now someone is trying to finish me off." He explained to an increasingly alarmed audience that they were dodging an assassin.

Schmidt quickly offered them his house for as long as they wished to stay. "A year . . . two years . . ."

McRae chuckled. "You're too generous, George."

"Not at all. We'll be the better for your company. Do you know what it's like to talk to horses' ears every day?" He squeezed his wife's hand. "Present company excepted, my dear."

She said, "Were you heading for New Orleans, General?"

"Yes . . . in a roundabout way."

"Well, why not stay here awhile, rest up. You do look a little pale, General."

Slocum said, "He's still recovering from a gunshot wound. I think it would be an excellent idea to rest up a bit more."

He had to explain the circumstances of the wound, and so it was decided they would stay on for a few days. Schmidt said, "We'll fatten you up."

It was a large house, with five bedchambers. Their children had grown up long since and moved out, Schmidt told them. "We rattle around in this big house, Marna and I. We generally close off four rooms . . ."

Slocum saw that the general was delighted to sleep in a bed each night and to be among old friends. It did make a difference, and Slocum did not mention moving on. After all, they had no timetable to respect.

And his only charge was to see the general was safe.

And he was quite safe here. How could anyone know where he was?

20

Frank Toms thought of nothing but the shining gold he'd seen in the prisoner's hands. To get it for himself, all he had to do was unlock the door and let the man out. He fingered the cell key and licked his lips.

Three hundred dollars in gold! He was sure no one in the entire town had ever possessed that much money all at one time! A man might work half a lifetime to amass it... saving pennies and scratching.

He could have it all, in one lump, in a minute!

And Stark was right. He'd step on board a steamboat, and the marshal would never see him again. Never yell at him or curse him again! Ever!

There was nothing in the town he wanted to take with him. No one to say good-bye to. He would be happy leaving the town behind, and especially happy with the gold eagles.

And the girls! Jesus! He had never dared let himself think of fondling a beautiful girl! Not one single girl in the entire area had ever given him a second glance. Not even at the dances. They all knew how poor he was, wearing patched clothes... with no money to spend on them... with no future...

But he could change all that in a moment. He was going to do it!

He made his regular round that evening, as always, and sat in the jail office as the marshal went to the Senate Saloon to drink and josh with his cronies . . . as *he* did every evening. "Sweep out this damn office while I'm gone, Frank."

He grinned at the marshal's back. He did not sweep the office; that was a victory of sorts. He waited patiently, and when the marshal looked in later, a little tipsy, he smiled. The marshal said, "Ever'thing all right, Frank?"

"Ever'thing's fine, Marshal. Good night."

" 'Night." The marshal grunted and left for home.

Frank walked up the street and had supper and came back with the prisoner's food on a tray. When there was no prisoner in the cells, he went home to his shack and ate out of a can.

He shoved the tray under the bars.

Stark said, "What about it, Frank?" He jingled the gold coins.

"All right, Mr. Stark. I'll do 'er. But we got to wait till late. Ever'one in town knows you're here."

Stark smiled and nodded. "Where's my horse?"

"Out back in the stable. I'll saddle 'im and bring 'im around front later."

"All right."

Frank got up his nerve. "Can I have some of the money now?"

Stark looked surprised. "Just as soon's you open this goddam cell door! Anything can happen till then."

Frank went back to the office, sighing. He'd had no real hope Stark would advance any money—but he wanted to feel that gold!

He sat by the office window, where any passerby could see him. He had to wait till the town was asleep. Then he'd open the cell and get his money—and hurry to the landing to wait for a steamboat. There was always one or two at night. He'd take the first one that came, no matter where it was bound.

There was nothing in his shack but a few cans of food. Nothing else he wanted. And he'd be glad to see the last of the town, and especially glad to see the last of the marshal.

He waited until eleven o'clock. He walked outside to the street and saw no lights at all; the town had gone to bed. What was there to keep any of them up? He walked to the stable, saddled Stark's horse, and led the animal around to the hitch rack in front.

Stark was impatient as hell in the cell, rapping on the bars. "Come on, unlock the goddam door, Frank!"

Frank put the key in the lock. "Your horse's out front."

Stark shoved the door open. "Where's my gun?"

"In the office on a hook."

Stark hurried into the office, pulled the Colt from the holster, and looked at the caps.

Frank said, "What about my money?"

"I left it in the cell, on the bed."

Frank turned and walked back quickly, with Stark behind him. As Frank entered the cell, Stark shot him twice and watched the body sprawl across the cot.

Then he locked the cell and tossed the keys inside.

By sunup he was far along the road, heading south. Before midday he was able to get across the river and felt safe. Now there would be more posters up for him, he was sure. But the more dangerous they made him appear, the less some honest citizen would try to confront him.

But of course being an armed and dangerous man had its backside. If a lawman located him, the law would probably collect a posse to surround him. Now that he'd killed two deputies, the law would never give up on him.

He didn't allow himself to dwell on that.

He came eventually to Grafton and took a room at the hotel, tired out. In the morning he wired for information and received the reply that there was none to give. Nothing at all had been heard from either Slocum or the general, not since Brewer.

He got out the map. Brewer wasn't that far away. It was just across the river and north a bit. So the general might still be in the vicinity.

But when he asked, no one seemed to have seen him.

A bartender said, "You lookin' for a general?" He laughed. "All's we got is a colonel. George Schmidt."

"The general I'm looking for was a Reb."

"So was Colonel George. He lives just out of town."

"That's interesting," Stark said. He finished his drink and went back to the hotel. It wasn't interesting at all. A man could spend his life listening to people talk about others who had been in the war.

The next morning he rode south again, to Lauren Hill. It was a large town, sprawling along a gentle hill, up from the river. It was the county seat, according to a sign. It had three hotels and eleven saloons. It took him a full day to talk to people in all of them. But no one could help him. If the general had been here, he had made no impression on anyone.

He stayed the night, feeling discouraged.

In the morning he saddled the horse and started south again. The road led through a newly landscaped area where there was a big new monument. A sprinkling of people were walking about, talking in small groups, and a few women were laying flowers at its base.

A half dozen buggies and a dozen saddled horses were in the road, and Stark had to weave his way through them. His path took him close to the monument, and he caught sight of a name carved on it—and reined in. General Butler McRae's name was near the top!

The monument was a register of all the men of the region who had served the Confederacy.

But the name that caught his attention was that of Colonel George Schmidt. It was just below McRae's, and both had served in the Twentieth Tennessee Volunteers. Schmidt was the man the bartender had mentioned! He lived near Grafton. So he and McRae had served together. That meant McRae might very well be a guest in Schmidt's home this instant! If he was close, the general was sure to look up an old friend.

Smiling, Stark turned about and headed back toward Grafton.

McRae and Schmidt played chess by the hour. George had had no one to play with for years. His wife did not care for the game, and his employees did not understand it, nor want to. They humored the colonel and let him win, which annoyed him.

Slocum spent his time riding about the farm or hunting in the surrounding woods. But there was little to hold his interest, and he quickly became restless and at loose ends. He rode into town, but it had little to offer beyond drink and cards . . . or women. He was not a drinker, nor did he care to play cards by the hour, and the women were mostly much older than he.

However, the weather steadily improved. The rains had gone, except for a drizzle or two now and then, and he was eager to get on to New Orleans.

One evening, after Slocum had come back from town, he and McRae walked out to the field beyond the barn, discussing future plans. McRae agreed that it was pleasant relaxing on the farm with Schmidt and his wife, but he felt more fit now than he had in a long while and was ready to depart.

"What do you suppose happened to Stark?"

Slocum shrugged. "No telling. I've watched for signs of him and seen nothing. I don't know how he could find out where we are . . ."

"No, I don't either."

The Schmidts were distressed when the general announced that, delightful as their stay had been, it was time to move on.

"You must come back," Schmidt said. "Stay half a year at least . . ."

McRae pressed his hand. "And have you beat me at chess constantly?"

"I promise not to."

Slocum said, "We have to return to San Francisco—as soon as this is over."

"Let's hope it's over now."

They saddled the horses in the morning, said their good-byes, and mounted to ride out, taking the road to town.

A half mile later, as the road entered the woods, the shot came, smashing the forehead of the general's horse. The animal went down in a threshing of legs, and McRae rolled free to lie motionless.

Slocum fired at the sudden blossom of smoke and circled his horse. "You all right, General?"

"I'm fine—never touched me." McRae sat up.

"Go back to the farm!" Slocum put spurs to the horse and galloped toward the slight bluff where the shot had come from.

As he reached it more shots came, seeking him out but missing widely. The sniper was on a horse—Slocum could hear the hoofbeats. He followed, wishing he had a rifle. The woods were thick, and he could not catch a glimpse of the other.

Then suddenly the woods ended, and he saw Stark—how could it be anyone but Stark? The man was far ahead, galloping a sorrel horse across a yellow field. The sorrel was a good mount and he could not close the distance.

How in hell had Stark found out where they were? The man must have a crystal ball! Did he have supernatural help? But of course, if he had, wouldn't his bullet have been guided to the general's chest instead of the horse's forehead?

He came to a cut through thick brush; it looked like a stage road, deeply rutted. The man he followed had gone that way and was out of sight in the turns. Slocum kept a close watch on the sides of the road. Stark might turn off at any time. It slowed him up, but it was necessary.

Then the brush thinned out, and there was a broad meadow to his left where, far off on the horizon, he saw the rider. Slocum turned after him.

After several miles he had to let up; the horse was blowing. He walked the animal, worrying that he'd lost Stark. The land was hilly and woodsy, and he caught glimpses of the other only now and then, moving generally in a straight line away. Slocum traversed bare brown ridges and grassy draws, watching for fresh prints. He looked at the sky—a long time till dark.

He was not closing, and he knew Stark would try one trick or another to lose him. And he might lie in an ambush. He had a rifle; it had been a rifle shot that had downed the general's horse. Slocum knew Stark had the advantage since he had to get close to use his pistol. He was wary about an ambush, and that slowed him, also.

Of course Stark did not know he had no rifle . . . was that an advantage? It might make Stark decide not to ambush him.

Maybe.

21

Stark left the monument behind and rode to Grafton. He had little trouble finding where Colonel George Schmidt lived. Apparently everyone in town knew him. The Schmidt family had lived there for ages. The war had not come to this part of the country, and his wife and the farm had survived intact. The estate was large, and Schmidt employed a dozen men from the town in various jobs. He had a large dairy herd and supplied the town with milk. He farmed, had orchards and horses, and traded outside the county.

As he sat in one of the town's deadfalls, Stark learned more about George Schmidt than he cared to know. The man was generally liked, and his business and personal life often became common knowledge because of it.

Stark's first visit to the farm was at night. He rode within sight of the buildings, then went forward on foot until a half dozen dogs began to howl. He retreated to his horse.

But no one came to see why the dogs were barking. Apparently they howled at odd sounds or forest animals as a matter of course. The next morning, Stark went as close as he dared and examined the farm buildings with binoculars. There was a large main house, many sheds and cribs, a bunkhouse, and a barn with several corrals. The entire area was fenced; the dogs were inside the fence.

Several times as he watched that morning, he saw the general and Slocum and a third man, who must be Colonel Schmidt, walking about under the trees, talking. They went into the barn and came out—all much too far for a rifle shot.

Well, Stark mused, they could not stay there forever. The day would come . . .

And he could not get to the house without the dogs' raising a racket. It was a standoff, as long as they remained in the Schmidt house.

He came to the same spot every day, watching. It was tiresome as hell, but he was finally rewarded. One morning he saw the horses saddled, embraces under the trees, then the general and Slocum rode out amid waves and took the road toward town.

Stark hurried to the spot he'd long since picked out as an ideal ambush site at a turn of the road. They would be coming directly toward him. He dropped prone in the tall weeds and looked along the rifle barrel, grinning.

When the two riders came in view, Stark centered on the general, putting the front sight on the man's chest.

He had paced off fifty yards and put a rock by the side of the road. When the riders reached the rock he fired. He saw the horse rear and fall and saw the general go sprawling—then Slocum was firing at him!

He had intended to hit the general, then shoot Slocum with the Colt. But Slocum was so damned fast and accurate! Bullets cut the weeds over his head, and Stark had to snake back down the rise, scramble to his horse, and spur away, swearing.

Half a mile away he looked back and saw that Slocum was following. If the general had been hurt, he would have stayed—probably. But not if the general was dead. So that meant the general was either unhurt or dead. Which? He had no idea.

SLOCUM AND THE RIVER CHASE   149

The sorrel was a strong, willing horse, and as the chase continued, he gained on Slocum. As soon as it got dark he'd turn abruptly to right or left, acccording to the land, and lose Slocum for good.

But damn, he'd have to return to Grafton, or near it, to find out whether he'd killed the general. If McRae was dead, it would appear in any local newspaper, he was positive.

He was walking the sorrel as it got dark, and as he began to cross a dry wash, he turned at right angles and followed along its shallow bank where brown brush was piled high. Looking back, he could not see his own tracks. He smiled in the night; Slocum would wander about now and never find him.

He rode most of the night and came back to Lauren Hill, arriving as the sun came up. He was dog tired and stiff, and he took a room at the town's cheapest hotel. The weekly would be out in four days, the clerk told him.

"But folks often asks at the office for news . . ."

"Where is the office?"

"Just 'round the corner. You'll see the sign."

Slocum lost the man on the sorrel horse when the sun went down. It gave him several choices. He could camp here on the trail and pick up the tracks in the morning, or he could give it all up and return to Schmidt's farm. Of course, if he went on he might get lucky and find himself forty feet from Stark at sunup.

But not likely.

And his job was to see that the general was safe. He decided to return.

He reached Lauren Hill several hours after dawn and had breakfast in a steamy little restaurant, then rode on to Grafton, arriving there the next day.

George Schmidt had heard the ambush shots and, with several men, had ridden along the road to find the general busy pulling the saddle off the dead horse.

Slocum had gone after the sniper, he told them, explaining what had happened.

"That man's been watching us at the farm!" Schmidt said.

"I'm afraid so."

"How in hell did he know you were here?"

McRae shook his head.

One of the men took the saddle, McRae climbed up behind Schmidt, and they returned to the house.

Slocum came riding in at dusk of the third day, looking unhappy. He had not gotten close to Stark and had had to give up the chase.

Over supper that night Schmidt asked, "Do you think that Stark fellow knows whether he hit you, General?"

"I don't know. I rolled free of the horse and stayed put. John fired back so fast that I'm sure Stark had to keep his head down. He might not know . . ."

Schmidt smiled broadly. "Then why don't we inform the local paper in Lauren Hill that General McRae has met with an unfortunate accident and has been buried—"

McRae shook his head.

"Why not?" Schmidt said. "It will keep him from coming back for a second try."

"I'd rather say nothing at all, George. The paper might fall into the hands of someone dear to me—or the item might be picked up by another paper."

"Very well . . ."

Slocum had seen the Wanted posters for Stark. They were tacked up in several places in town. His price had increased since he'd shot the second deputy. Stark was now worth $750 dead or alive.

Schmidt said, "Then he won't be able to walk the streets."

"But it's possible he'll come back to Grafton," Slocum replied. "I'll bet he doesn't know if the general is alive or not."

"Then you can stay here awhile," Schmidt said, rubbing his hands.

"We ought to go—Stark or no Stark, George. I'm getting itchy about returning to San Francisco."

"If you must," Schmidt said with resignation.

"We can go into Grafton late," Slocum said. "We'll leave the horses behind and take the first steamboat south. With any luck at all, Stark will be nowhere about."

McRae nodded and Schmidt agreed. "All right, we'll take the buggy. It'll hold the three of us fine. When d'you want to go?"

"Tonight," Slocum said.

An hour after dark they said their good-byes again to Marna and climbed in the buggy. Schmidt drove them into town, taking a back alley when they reached its outskirts.

They waited nearly two hours near the landing before a steamboat arrived, brightly lighted, puffing steam. It was a smaller stern-wheeler; it put off a dozen boxes and barrels as Slocum and McRae boarded, and was off again as the whistle blew three blasts.

George Schmidt stood on the landing, waving as the boat slipped into the stream.

They saw no sign of Stark.

22

Buford Stark had gotten careless in Grafton; he had seen none of the posters for several days and had gone into the Commerce Saloon for a drink. Standing at the bar, he had noticed, in the back bar mirror, a man who seemed interested in him. Turning slightly, Stark saw the man wore a badge. When the man was distracted a moment, Stark left his drink on the bar and slipped out to the street, climbed on his horse, and hurried out of town.

The deputy ran out and watched him disappear in the night. He then went to the telegraph office and wired the marshal in Lauren Hill to be on the lookout for Stark.

Lauren Hill, the county seat, was a large town. Stark did not enter on the road from Grafton but circled through the fields and came in from the east. He rode up and down several streets till he found a boardinghouse sign and registered as Henry Acker from Council Bluffs. He was on his way home, he told the owner, where a job awaited him, starting in the summer.

The house owner, Jack Herald, had heard that story or one very like it for years and did not give his boarder a second thought, other than to get the room rent in advance.

When the weekly appeared, Stark bought a copy and read it from front to back. There was no mention of McRae at all. At supper he discussed newspapers with Herald, who proved to be a believer in nothing. Sometimes, Herald said, it took weeks for news to get printed.

Stark then wired for information, saying he was in Lauren Hill. Had the general reported in?

The reply came quickly. He had not. "What are you doing about it?"

Stark wired that he had a farm under surveillance where he believed the general to be staying. He did not mention the shooting.

And he did not wait for another reply but left at once for Grafton. It took several days to return to his nook by the farm, but in three days of watching he did not see either the general or Slocum. It made him uneasy—except their horses were in the near corral.

Maybe he had wounded McRae. Perhaps he was in bed, slowly sinking...

That thought made him feel much better.

However, keeping watch on the Schmidt farm was not only difficult, it was monotonous in the extreme. He had rented a room in Grafton, telling the woman owner that he was waiting for his brother to arrive. He left early in the mornings and returned usually after dark.

In a week the Lauren Hill *Clarion* was brought into town. Stark bought a copy and read it front to back. In a gossip column he was startled to read that General Butler McRae was a guest in the home of friends in the lovely Crescent City, New Orleans.

Stark gaped at the few lines. McRae in New Orleans? Jesus Christ! Here he was, guarding a damned farmhouse in the sticks. Slocum and the general had stolen a march on him. And McRae was probably not wounded at all.

He packed his few possessions, sold his horse to the

liveryman, and boarded a steamboat, furious at the turn events had taken. He paced the decks, growling to himself. New Orleans was a great city. Where in it would McRae be staying? Did he have relatives there? Maybe members of the Twentieth Tennessee Volunteers. Where in hell would he begin to look?

But the newspaper had gotten the news he was in town—maybe they could tell him. They had reporters snooping everywhere.

He had begun to look more than a little ragged, what with lying about in the woods for days on end. On the boat he noticed people looking at him sidelong and whispering behind their hands, and as soon as he arrived in New Orleans he bought new clothes and tossed the old duds away. He also bought a pair of gold-rimmed glasses, with plain glass, as camouflage. He had not seen any posters on the steamboat and did not notice any in the city. There must be new posters issued every day. Probably his were now covered by others.

His next move was suggested by an ad in the first newspaper he bought. A detective agency advertised its services as tracers and information gatherers. Its address was on Boudin Street. Stark went there at once.

It was a small office, opening off the street. When he turned the knob and went in, a middle-aged man with a black mustache and glossy black hair rose from behind a desk with a newspaper in his hand.

"What can I do for you, sir?"

"Are you the detective?"

"I am." He pointed to a chair. "My name is Collins. Francis Collins, at your service, retired from the New Orleans force."

"Ahhhh, an ex-policeman."

"Yes sir. And it helps now and then. Is it divorce business you have in mind?"

"No. I want you to find someone for me. My name is Henry Acker."

"I see. And are you certain this person is now in New Orleans?"

"Yes. It was mentioned in the paper."

"Ahhh. Then we should be able to locate him." Collins wetted a pencil. "Where are you living, Mr. Acker?"

The threat from Stark seemed to be over, if only because he could not find them. Their journey downriver to New Orleans had probably gone unnoticed by him. He could not watch every boat at every town. Despite a very close watch, Slocum could detect no curious eyes or followers.

They had taken rooms at a small neighborhood hotel, and McRae had kept busy attending various gatherings of wartime comrades and their families. He was in demand as a casual speaker.

Slocum insisted on taking precautions with his safety, even though he was reasonably sure their presence in the city was not known to Stark.

"How in the world could he know?" McRae asked.

"He might find out," Slocum replied stubbornly. "How did he know we were at the Schmidt farm?"

"Perhaps he was lucky."

"Then he might get lucky again. I think we should take a ship to San Francisco. We could watch everyone who came aboard and be certain."

McRae sighed deeply. "Ships are not my favorite method of travel. I get seasick on the water."

"Then we'll go back upriver, maybe all the way to Omaha, and take a train from there. No one gets seasick on the river."

McRae smiled. "I vote for that."

The general was eager to get back to San Francisco because the manuscript of his memoirs was due in his publisher's office—overdue, in fact. The time they had agreed for its completion had gone past. McRae wired for an extension, explaining the problem he faced; he had not contemplated this long journey but now had reason to believe it had come to an end. The publisher wired back, allowing the extension.

They packed their belongings and prepared to take a steamboat upriver.

There were a number of Confederate organizations in New Orleans that held socials and dances. Some provided help and hospitalization for veterans, since the federal government did not offer services to ex-Rebels. Francis Collins went through these groups methodically, asking about General Butler McRae.

A great many had heard of him, but it took almost a week to find someone who had seen the general recently. He had attended a reunion of Alabama cavalrymen, a group headed by ex-Colonel Norton Fisher.

Collins traced Fisher to a house on Laville Street and was introduced to the colonel, a wiry, intense-looking man who had just come in from playing baseball in a nearby field. Yes, he had talked with General McRae only two days past.

"Can you tell me where I can find him?"

"Why do you want to see him? Is there trouble?"

"No trouble." Collins repeated the story Stark had told him. "I have a client who owns property with McRae and wants to sell his share, but he needs McRae's permission."

"I see." Fisher nodded and looked in a notebook, then shook his head. "I don't have an address, but I know he lives in a hotel somewhere near Butrand Square—do you know it? The one with the statue and the fountain."

"Yes, I know the square." Collins rose. "Thank you, Colonel."

Back in the office, Collins sent a messenger to his client, detailing what he had learned.

Stark went at once to Butrand Square and discovered there were five hotels in the vicinity. He went to each one, asking his questions. At the fourth he received a yes.

"The two men you are looking for left early yesterday morning." The clerk was sorry. "You missed them by only a few hours."

"Do you know where they went?"

The clerk shrugged. "I think they were bound for St. Louis."

Stark rushed to the river and got passage on the first boat headed north.

23

The passage to St. Louis on the magnificent steamer, *Lotus*, was uneventful. It was a floating palace with crystal chandeliers, red plush divans, much gilt and scarlet, and food like the best restaurants.

In St. Louis they took rooms in a hotel near the waterfront. Slocum hunted down a telegraph office and sent wires to Reardon and Munch saying they were in good health and returning to San Francisco. They would of course stop in Omaha to see Reardon.

They had seen the last of the great steamboats and had to buy tickets on a small stern-wheeler for the trip upriver through Kansas City. The *Columbia* was a small boat, packed with cargo for merchants hundreds of miles north of Omaha at Bismarck on the upper reaches of the Missouri.

There were nine passengers, other than Slocum and the general, all men; some were miners, and some merchants and drummers. The crew was small, and the boat bustled along at a steady pace. There was no fancy lounge or accomplished chef. The food, compared to that on the *Lotus*, was poor and meager, the staterooms were stuffy and uncomfortable cubicles, the beds narrow. Cargo paid much more than passengers—and did not complain.

There was little for a passenger to do but stay out of the way. One might eat and drink, play cards, or chatter. Or he might sleep away the hours. He might even lean on the guardrails and chew cigars while he watched the shoreline change as it glided by, with birds wheeling across the sky in a dazzle of sunshine.

The boat stopped often for wood, which the roustabouts piled high on the main deck near the fireboxes as they chanted their work songs. It stopped too at towns to deliver cargo or take it on, and occasionally a passenger got off with his carpetbag, or another boarded.

The general slept a good deal, and they were both glad to walk across the gangplank at Kansas City nearly four days later. The boat would tie up for a few hours, the mate told them, then go on till dark. They never ran after dark on the upper river.

It was a close, heavy afternoon of sunshine, and the river was veiled by a silvery haze. McRae's entire attitude had changed, Slocum thought. The other seemed much more relaxed now that they were on the return trip—and Stark had been left far behind. Their constant vigilance had been modified. Slocum examined the passengers who boarded, but none had resembled Stark in the slightest.

They had supper in a restaurant and returned to the boat. The several hours mentioned by the mate had turned into double that, and now that dusk was approaching, the mate said, they would not leave until morning at the earliest. Several of the wooden paddles had been damaged by a floating log and were being replaced. It was one of the ordinary incidents of river travel. A work crew would labor by lantern light until they were finished.

Slocum and the general walked the levee in the fading light. They would take the Union Pacific Railroad at Omaha and be in San Francisco in a few days, Slocum said.

The general nodded. "I wish it were tomorrow."

• • •

Buford Stark reached St. Louis in time to see the two men he sought get on a small stern-wheeler, the *Columbia*. There was no possibility of boarding it himself—without a gun battle. He was positive Slocum would look at every passenger, and the boat was too small to carry many.

But he was jubilant that he had located them. It was the first bit of luck to come his way for a while . . . though he told himself it was not luck but diligence.

He was certain now that they were returning to San Francisco.

Stark sent off a telegram to say he was closing in—and received a reply that he must do so at once.

His first order of business was to hire two helpers. In the Commerce Saloon he met the Sewell brothers and talked to them for an hour or more over beer and cigars. They were a pair of big, heavyset men in their early forties both recently arrived from the East, where they were wanted in half a dozen states for various felonies, especially armed robbery.

Yes, they both owned rifles, and they were willing to pretend to be hunters if need be. Stark promised that when they caught up with the general and disposed of him, they would be paid in gold. They liked the sound of that.

Stark had already hired a small steam packet, and his plan was simple. They would follow the *Columbia*, and when it was well away from any habitation they would board it, run it aground, and dispose of both Slocum and the general.

Three of them should be able to do it efficiently. The Sewell brothers thought so, too. They also discussed going through the pockets of any passengers on the *Columbia*, and Stark merely shrugged. That was an extra.

The small packet was owned and run by Elias Hupp, a lean, weathered riverman who had spent many years transporting illegal whiskey up and down the river. He declared his boat could easily outrun most other boats; the speed was what kept him in the trade.

Stark and the two brothers boarded the boat, and Hupp got steam up.

Stark said nothing about attacking the *Columbia*, knowing the riverman would refuse. The captain of the *Columbia*, and maybe others, would recognize the small packet at once and would be able to say so in court.

But after several hours, as they followed the steamboat upriver, Stark pushed Hupp into a corner. "Now, Mr. Hupp, you will lay us alongside the *Columbia*. We're going to board her."

Hupp was startled, having been told they were hunters. "You goin' to rob her? That's Jim Regan's boat!"

"I don't care whose boat it is." Stark showed the man his revolver. "You lay us alongside."

Hupp eyed the gun and the two big men with rifles and sighed. He had been on the shady side of the law too long not to recognize serious men. He would lose the boat if he did not do as he was told . . . and possibly his life as well.

Stark said, "You approach her like you're going to pass by—then you come in quickly and we'll jump aboard."

Hupp nodded. It was a damn poor plan. The people on the other boat would be watching if they came that close! Obviously Stark knew nothing about boats, and Hupp wasn't about to give him lessons.

Stark said, "We'll be behind these bulkheads, and you will give us the word when it's time to jump."

"All right." What else could he do? He'd turn the boat about and get the hell out as soon as they jumped.

Stark cocked the revolver menacingly. "Do it right and nothing will happen to you. Otherwise you go into the river. Understand?"

"I get you." Hupp believed him.

The *Columbia* had steam up at dawn and backed into the stream with three blasts of the whistle. Someone was singing the riverman's song, "Good-bye, Little Girl, Good-bye."

Captain Regan walked through the main salon as they headed upstream. On the foredeck he watched the sun sparkling on the water. He was always glad to head for his home in Omaha. He would be able to spend several nights with his wife . . .

They passed several boats, small craft that had put out from the shore. Now and then they saw men fishing close to the opposite tree-lined bank.

Then Slocum noticed the boat following.

He pointed it out to Regan, who squinted at it. "Looks like Elias Hupp's boat. Wonder what he's doin' up thisaway. He's usual headin' south."

"You know him?"

"Hell, I know most ever'one on the goddam river. I been on it all m'life. Elias, he makes a livin' running whiskey at night. Tha's why he don't come up here much."

"He runs whiskey?"

Regan grinned. "Lots of folks do. To beat the tax."

Slocum studied the approaching steamer. It was obviously much faster than the *Columbia*. It might have to be if the owner carried illegal goods for a living. It would have to be able to outrun the law.

He pointed out the boat to the general, who was curious. "You think Stark might be aboard?"

"I'm suspicious of anything out of the ordinary," Slocum confessed. "Captain Regan knows the boat and says it seldom comes upriver."

"What do you want to do?"

Slocum frowned at the distant boat. "I think we ought to go up to the wheelhouse. There's no way we could defend the entire boat. He might have a gang with him." He glanced at the sky. "And we need a rifle."

"I'll ask the captain if he has one."

"Good. And a spare pistol, too."

Captain Regan was startled at the request. "There's going to be shootin'?"

"There might be." McRae spoke earnestly. "If that boat

carries the man we think it does, there probably will be. He wants my hide."

"He wants to kill you?"

McRae nodded.

"All right." Regan sighed deeply. "I got a rifle. Another pistol, too." He led the way to his cabin and handed them over, with ammunition. He had a Winchester and a Remington pistol. McRae carried them up to the wheelhouse, where a wide-eyed pilot stared at him.

Slocum was there, talking to the pilot. "Can you keep that boat from closing with us?"

"I doubt it. He's much faster—and it's a narrow channel. You think he's going to come in close?"

"Probably. Could he force us to the bank?"

"No. But he can come in. This boat's ninety feet long. It ain't a puppy wagging its tail."

"All right. But do what you can to keep them from boarding us too easily." He took the Winchester from the general and examined the magazine. It was fully loaded.

McRae asked the pilot, "How long do you think it will take them to come up to us?"

The man had a ready answer, having kept an eye on the boat. "Probably an hour." He paused and glanced at Slocum. "But if they're going to board, they may start shooting first.

Slocum agreed. "They'll shoot at you, here in the wheelhouse, to stop the boat. Be ready to duck."

The pilot looked pale as he nodded. He had already thought of that.

Slocum went out to the deck and walked to the stern, past the tied-down yawl, and gazed at the approaching boat. He could see no one aboard. It was a small, sleek steamer, painted black, and looked ominous. How many did Stark have with him—if it was Stark?

He fingered the rifle as he gazed at the boat. If he started shooting and Stark was not aboard, there might be hell to pay. Would Reardon go his bail? His reasons might sound outrageous to a judge.

He returned to the pilothouse and the pilot said, "We're coming to a long reach. He'll be on us in half an hour."

McRae asked, "What's a reach?"

"A long, straight run of river. He'll gain on us there."

Slocum said, "When they get within rifle range they'll shoot at you. Be ready for it. I'll be aft, shooting back at them—it may discourage them a bit."

"Don't take chances, John . . ."

Slocum smiled. "I never gave orders to a general before. But you lie on the deck. It's the safest place, because they'll be shooting upward."

McRae glanced at the pilot. "We understand."

The pilot groaned. "How the hell did I ever get into this!"

24

Slocum lay prone on the afterdeck with the Winchester, watching the boat approach. He could make out the form of one man at the wheel but no one else. The crew must be hiding, and Stark, if he was there, was probably behind the forward bulkheads. The pilot would be able to tell him when the boat was crowding the *Columbia*.

Taking careful aim, he squeezed the trigger and sent a shot just over the small wheelhouse. It whacked into something and sent splinters flying. But the boat did not swerve. The pilot disappeared from view, and Slocum's next shot smashed the window glass.

Arms appeared and pistol shots suddenly erupted. Bullets sprayed the side of the *Columbia* in a wild fusillade that smashed the pilothouse windows and *spang*ed off into the sky.

Then the black boat nudged the *Columbia*.

Slocum snaked out the Colt and fired at the first man who jumped up from behind the bulkheads. He saw the man stagger and fall back—it was not Stark—but then two others dashed across to the *Columbia*'s main deck. In seconds they were out of sight.

He hurried back to the pilothouse, stood the rifle in a corner, and pulled a second pistol.

McRae looked questioningly and Slocum said, "Two of them on board. One is Stark. Watch the other side."

McRae nodded.

To get to them on the hurricane deck the attackers would have to come up the fore ladder or climb up one of the uprights along the boat's side. It was a large area to watch.

Several shots sounded below them on the boiler deck. Possibly the boarders were herding the crew and passengers together, out of the way.

The main stairs were forward near the tall smokestacks, and Slocum kept an eye on them. The boat was gradually slowing, and he realized he had not heard the clang of the firebox doors for a while. The firemen were not feeding the boiler fires, and the boat was losing steam.

He walked along the edge of the deck, peering down. He could hear a babble of voices. The big stern wheel was definitely slowing.

McRae suddenly fired, and Slocum ran past the pilothouse. McRae pointed. He had fired at someone near the stairs. Instinctively Slocum whirled about and saw one of the men climbing to the deck by the steam escape pipe. Slocum snapped a shot at him, and the man ducked.

The two boarders had separated, and only Slocum's quick action had saved one of them from firing. He motioned the general back into the pilothouse. All the glass was out of the windows, and the pilot was on his knees, peeking out to keep the boat in the channel. He turned a chalky face toward them, eyes round. Slocum gave him a reassuring smile.

McRae asked, "You're sure there's only two of them?"

"There were three. But one's still on the other boat."

The general nodded.

Slocum said to the pilot, "Move the boat out of the channel and nudge the bank—keep her there."

"All right." The man turned the wheel, and the boat

moved clumsily, stopping in slack water, the stern wheel no longer turning.

Slocum studied the sky. Another three or four hours till dark. Would Stark and his helper charge them or wait? Maybe they were waiting for night.

Maybe he could get the general off the boat.

Nothing happened for two hours. The pilot picked up shards of glass from the deck and tossed them into the river.

McRae said softly, "What'll we do when it gets dark?"

"Try to get ashore without them seeing. They can't watch everywhere. Maybe we can climb down to the main deck." To the pilot he said, "They don't want you. Stay here and keep your head down."

"D-don't worry . . ."

There was no moon. Slocum made a turn about the shadowy deck, moving silently. Aft, by the yawl, he lay flat, listening. He could hear voices from the salon, and the muted sounds of the river; frogs were croaking in the mud nearby. No one seemed to be near.

He brought the general to the spot and climbed down with utmost caution to the cabin deck. With a pistol in each hand he waited as the general came down with rather more agility than he expected. They were on the river side of the boat, and it was a temptation to slide over the guardrails and slip into the dark water. He would have done it if he'd been alone. But the general had admitted he was a poor swimmer.

They were at the end of the cabins, and he pointed toward the land side and moved that way, silent as an Indian. They crossed the boat, and Slocum halted to look along the deck toward the fireboxes.

A shadow detached itself and a voice said, "Stark?"

Slocum said, "Yes . . ." But the other fired. A blossom of flame and a bullet splintered the bulkhead near his head. He had made the wrong reply. He motioned to McRae to lie flat on the deck and moved away toward the stern, watching both sides of the boat. The man who fired had been on the left; he was not Stark.

In a moment he saw movement on the river side. He was about to fire when the man on the left appeared at the end of the cabin and fired again. The shot slammed into the toilets, and Slocum fired twice and fell flat. He saw the man whirl about, then a shot came from Stark.

Slocum rolled and fired twice, then got up and ran toward Stark, firing again and again.

Stark was hurled back against the guardrails. He fired into the deck, then the pistol slipped out of his hand and clattered away. He fell in a heap.

When Slocum reached him he was dead.

The other man was dead also. A paper on his body said he was Amos Sewell.

The black steamer had disappeared. Captain Regan said they probably wouldn't locate him for a year. "Old Hupp knows every goddam nook and cranny in this river."

They found a telegraph form on Stark's body. It had been sent from San Francisco. It ordered Stark to pursue the general.

When they got to Omaha and were in Reardon's office, Reardon said, "This had to come from Munch. Every wire I received was sealed when it came into my hands, and my only staff is Mrs. Shepard, who is a copyist and in her seventies."

Slocum said, "Then it's your move from here."

Reardon nodded. "I'll be going to San Francisco with the general. We'll confront Giles Munch—with Lieutenant Pike."

Epilogue

Giles Munch was forced to admit he was the man behind certain guerrilla actions during the war. He was sent back to Kentucky, where he was tried and convicted of war crimes.

A sentence of death was carried out.

RICHARD MATHESON
author of DUEL

is back with his most exciting Western yet!

JOURNAL OF THE GUN YEARS

Clay Halser is the fastest gun west of the Mississippi, and he's captured the fancy of newspapermen and pulp writers back East. That's good news for Halser, but bad news for the endless army of young tinhorns who ride into town to challenge him and die by his gun. As Halser's body count grows, so does his legend. Worse, he's starting to believe his own publicity—which could ultimately prove deadly!

*Turn the page
for an exciting chapter from*

JOURNAL OF THE GUN YEARS

by
Richard Matheson

On sale now,
wherever Berkley Books are sold!

BOOK ONE
(1864–1867)

It is my unhappy lot to write the closing entry in this journal.

Clay Halser is dead, killed this morning in my presence.

I have known him since we met during the latter days of The War Between The States. I have run across him, on occasion, through ensuing years and am, in fact, partially responsible (albeit involuntarily) for a portion of the legend which has magnified around him.

It is for these reasons (and another more important) that I make this final entry.

I am in Silver Gulch acquiring research matter toward the preparation of a volume on the history of this territory (Colorado), which has recently become the thirty-eighth state of our Union.

I was having breakfast in the dining room of the *Silver Lode Hotel* when a man entered and sat down at a table across the room, his back to the wall. Initially, I failed to recognize him though there was, in his comportment, something familiar.

Several minutes later (to my startlement), I realized that it was none other than Clay Halser. True, I had not laid eyes on him for many years. Nonetheless, I was completely taken back by the change in his appearance.

I was not, at that point, aware of his age, but took it to be somewhere in the middle thirties. Contrary to this, he presented the aspect of a man at least a decade older.

His face was haggard, his complexion (in my memory, quite ruddy) pale to the point of being ashen. His eyes, formerly suffused with animation, now looked burned out, dead. What many horrific sights those eyes had beheld I could not—and cannot—begin to estimate. Whatever those sights, however, no evidence of them had been reflected in his eyes before; it was as though he'd been emotionally immune.

He was no longer so. Rather, one could easily imagine that his eyes were gazing, in that very moment, at those bloody sights, dredging from the depths within his mind to which he'd relegated them, all their awful measure.

From the standpoint of physique, his deterioration was equally marked. I had always known him as a man of vigorous health, a condition necessary to sustain him in the execution of his harrowing duties. He was not a tall man; I would gauge his height at five feet ten inches maximum, perhaps an inch or so less, since his upright carriage and customary dress of black suit, hat, and boots might have afforded him the look of standing taller than he did. He had always been extremely well-presented though, with a broad chest, narrow waist, and pantherlike grace of movement; all in all, a picture of vitality.

Now, as he ate his meal across from me, I felt as though, by some bizarre transfiguration, I was gazing at an old man.

He had lost considerable weight and his dark suit (it, too, seemed worn and past its time) hung loosely on his frame. To my further disquiet, I noted a threading of gray through his dark blonde hair and saw a tremor in his hands completely foreign to the young man I had known.

I came close to summary departure. To my shame, I nearly chose to leave rather than accost him. Despite the congenial relationship I had enjoyed with him throughout the past decade, I found myself so totally dismayed by the alteration in his looks that I lacked the will to rise and cross the room to him, preferring to consider hasty exit. (I discovered, later, that the reason he had failed to notice me was that his vision, always so acute before, was now inordinately weak.)

At last, however, girding up my will, I stood and moved across the dining room, attempting to fix a smile of pleased surprise on my lips and hoping he would not be too aware of my distress.

"Well, good morning, Clay," I said, as evenly as possible.

I came close to baring my deception at the outset for, as he looked up sharply at me, his expression one of taut alarm, a perceptible "tic" under his right eye, I was hard put not to draw back apprehensively.

Abruptly, then, he smiled (though it was more a ghost of the smile I remembered). *"Frank,"* he said and jumped to his feet. No, that is not an accurate description of his movement. It may well have been his intent to jump up and welcome me with avid handshake. As it happened, his stand was labored, his hand grip lacking in strength. "How *are* you?" he inquired. "It is good to see you."

"I'm fine," I answered.

"Good." He nodded, gesturing toward the table. "Join me."

I hope my momentary hesitation passed his notice. "I'd be happy to," I told him.

"Good," he said again.

We each sat down, he with his back toward the wall again. As we did, I noted how his gaunt frame slumped into the chair, so different from the movement of his earlier days.

He asked me if I'd eaten breakfast.

"Yes." I pointed across the room. "I was finishing when you entered."

"I am glad you came over," he said.

There was a momentary silence. Uncomfortable, I tried to think of something to say.

He helped me out. (I wonder, now, if it was deliberate; if he had, already, taken note of my discomfort.) "Well, old fellow," he asked, "what brings you to this neck of the woods?"

I explained my presence in Silver Gulch and, as I did, being now so close to him, was able to distinguish, in detail, the astounding metamorphosis which time (and experience) had effected.

There seemed to be, indelibly impressed on his still handsome face, a look of unutterable sorrow. His former blitheness had completely vanished and it was oppressive to behold what had occurred to his expression, to see the palsied gestures of his hands as he spoke, perceive the constant shifting of his eyes as though he was anticipating that, at any second, some impending danger might be thrust upon him.

I tried to coerce myself not to observe these things, concentrating on the task of bringing him "up to date" on my activities since last we'd met; no match for his activities, God knows.

"What about you?" I finally asked; I had no more to say about myself. "What are you doing these days?"

"Oh, gambling," he said, his listless tone indicative of his regard for that pursuit.

"No marshaling anymore?" I asked.

He shook his head. "Strictly the circuit," he answered.

"Circuit?" I wasn't really curious but feared the onset of silence and spoke the first word that occurred to me.

"A league of boomtown havens for faro players," he replied. "South Texas up to South Dakota—Idaho to Arizona. There is money to be gotten everywhere. Not that I am good enough to make a raise. And not that it's important if I do, at any rate. I only gamble for something to do."

All the time he spoke, his eyes kept shifting, searching; was it *waiting*?

As silence threatened once again, I quickly spoke. "Well, you have traveled quite a long road since the War," I said. "A long, exciting road." I forced a smile. *"Adventurous,"* I added.

His answering smile was as sadly bitter and exhausted as any I have ever witnessed. "Yes, the writers of the stories have made it all sound very colorful," he said. He leaned back with a heavy sigh, regarding me. "I even thought it so myself at one time. Now I recognize it all for what it was." There was a tightening around his eyes. "Frank, it was drab, and dirty, and there was a lot of blood."

I had no idea how to respond to that and, in spite of my resolve, let silence fall between us once more.

Silence broke in a way that made my flesh go cold. A young man's voice behind me, from some distance in the room. "So that is him," the voice said loudly. "Well, he does not look like much to me."

I'd begun to turn when Clay reached out and gripped my arm. "Don't bother looking," he instructed me. "It's best to ignore them. I have found the more attention paid, the more difficult they are to shake in the long run."

He smiled but there was little humor in it. "Don't be concerned," he said. "It happens all the time. They spout a while, then go away, and brag that Halser took their guff and never did a thing. It makes them feel important. I don't mind. I've grown accustomed to it."

At which point, the boy—I could now tell, from the timbre of his voice, that he had not attained his majority—spoke again.

"He looks like nothing at all to me to be so all-fired famous a fighter with his guns," he said.

I confess the hostile quaver of his voice unsettled me. Seeing my reaction, Clay smiled and was about to speak when the boy—perhaps seeing the smile and angered by it—added, in a tone resounding enough to be heard in the lobby, "In fact, I believe he looks like a woman-hearted coward, that is what he looks like to me!"

"Don't worry now," Clay reassured me. "He'll blow himself out of steam presently and crawl away." I felt some sense of relief to see a glimmer of the old sauce in his eyes. "Probably to visit, with uncommon haste, the nearest outhouse."

Still, the boy kept on with stubborn malice. "My name is Billy Howard," he announced. "And I am going to make . . ."

He went abruptly mute as Clay unbuttoned his dark frock coat to reveal a butt-reversed Colt at his left side. It was little wonder. Even I, a friend of Clay's, felt a chill of premonition at the movement. What spasm of dread it must have caused in the boy's heart, I can scarcely imagine.

"Sometimes I have to go this far," Clay told me. "Usually I wait longer but, since you are with me . . ." He let the sentence go unfinished and lifted his cup again.

I wanted to believe the incident was closed but, as we spoke—me asking questions to distract my mind from its foreboding state—I seemed to feel the presence of the boy behind me like some constant wraith.

"How are all your friends?" I asked.

"Dead," Clay answered.

"*All* of them?"

He nodded. "Yes. Jim Clements. Ben Pickett. John Harris." I saw a movement in his throat. "Henry Blackstone. All of them."

I had some difficulty breathing. I kept expecting to hear the boy's voice again. "What about your wife?" I asked.

"I have not heard from her in some time," he replied. "We are estranged."

"How old is your daughter now?"

"Three in January," he answered, his look of sadness deepening. I regretted having asked and quickly said, "What about your family in Indiana?"

"I went back to visit them last year," he said. "It was a waste."

I did not want to know, but heard myself inquiring nonetheless, "Why?"

"Oh . . . what I have become," he said. "What journalists have made me. Not you," he amended, believing, I suppose, that he'd insulted me. "My reputation, I mean. It stood like a wall between my family and me. I don't think they saw me. Not *me*. They saw what they believed I am."

The voice of Billy Howard made me start. "Well, why does he just *sit* there?" he said.

Clay ignored him. Or, perhaps, he did not even hear, so deep was he immersed in black thoughts.

"Hickok was right," he said, "I am not a man anymore. I'm a figment of imagination. Do you know, I looked at my reflection in the mirror this morning and did not even know who I was looking at? Who is that staring at me? I wondered. Clay Halser of Pine Grove? Or the *Hero of The Plains*?" he finished with contempt.

"Well?" demanded Billy Howard. "Why *does* he?"

Clay was silent for a passage of seconds and I felt my muscles drawing in, anticipating God knew what.

"I had no answer for my mirror," he went on then. "I have no answers left for anyone. All I know is that I am tired. They have offered me the job of City Marshal here and, although I could use the money, I cannot find it in myself to accept."

Clay Halser stared into my eyes and told me quietly, "To answer your long-time question: yes, Frank, I have learned what fear is. Though not fear of . . ."

He broke off as the boy spoke again, his tone now venomous. "I think he is afraid of me," said Billy Howard.

Clay drew in a long, deep breath, then slowly shifted his gaze to look across my shoulder. I sat immobile, conscious of an air of tension in the entire room now, everyone waiting with held breath.

"That is what I think," the boy's voice said. "I think Almighty God Halser is afraid of me."

Clay said nothing, looking past me at the boy. I did not dare to turn. I sat there, petrified.

"I think the Almighty God Halser is a yellow skunk!" cried Billy Howard. "I think he is a murderer who shoots men in the back and will not . . . !"

The boy's voice stopped again as Clay stood so abruptly that I felt a painful jolting in my heart. "I'll be right back," he said.

He walked past me and, shuddering, I turned to watch. It had grown so deathly still in the room that, as I did, the legs of my chair squeaked and caused some nearby diners to start.

I saw, now, for the first time, Clay Halser's challenger and was aghast at the callow look of him. He could not have been more than sixteen years of age and might well have been younger, his face speckled with skin blemishes, his dark hair long and shaggy. He was poorly dressed and had an old six-shooter pushed beneath the waistband of his faded trousers.

I wondered vaguely whether I should move, for I was sitting in whatever line of fire the boy might direct. I wondered vaguely if the other diners were wondering the same thing. If they were, their limbs were as frozen as mine.

I heard every word exchanged by the two.

"Now don't you think that we have had enough of this?" Clay said to the boy. "These folks are having their breakfast and I think that we should let them eat their meal in peace."

"Step out into the street then," said the boy.

"Now why should I step out into the street?" Clay asked. I knew it was no question. He was doing what he could to calm the agitated boy—that agitation obvious as the boy replied, "To fight me with your gun."

"You don't want to fight me," Clay informed him. "You would just be killed and no one would be better for it."

"You mean *you* don't want to fight *me*," the youth retorted. Even from where I sat, I could see that his face was almost white; it was clear that he was terror-stricken.

Still, he would not allow himself to back off, though Clay was giving him full opportunity. "*You* don't want to fight *me*," he repeated.

"That is not the case at all," Clay replied. "It is just that I am tired of fighting."

"I *thought* so!" cried the boy with malignant glee.

"Look," Clay told him quietly, "if it will make you feel good, you are free to tell your friends, or anyone you choose, that I backed down from you. You have my permission to do that."

"I don't need your d———d permission," snarled the boy. With a sudden move, he scraped his chair back, rising to feet. Unnervingly, he seemed to be gaining resolution rather than losing it—as though, in some way, he sensed the weakness in Clay, despite the fact that Clay was famous for his prowess with the handgun. "I am sick of listening to you," he declared. "Are you going to step outside with me and pull your gun like a man, or do I shoot you down like a dog?"

"Go *home*, boy," Clay responded—and I felt an icy grip of premonition strike me full force as his voice broke in the middle of a word.

"Pull, you yellow b———d," Billy Howard ordered him.

Several diners close to them lunged up from their tables, scattering for the lobby. Clay stood motionless.

"I said *pull*, you God d———d son of a b———h!" Billy Howard shouted.

"No," was all Clay Halser answered.

"Then *I* will!" cried the boy.

Before his gun was halfway from the waistband of his trousers, Clay's had cleared its holster. Then—with what capricious twist of fate!—his shot misfired and, before he could squeeze off another, the boy's gun had discharged and a bullet struck Clay full in the chest, sending him reeling back to hit a table, then sprawl sideways to the floor.

Through the pall of dark smoke, Billy Howard gaped down at his victim. "I did it," he muttered. "I *did* it." Though chance alone had done it.

Suddenly, his pistol clattered to the floor as his fingers lost their holding power and, with a cry of what he likely thought was victory, he bolted from the room. (Later, I heard, he was killed in a knife fight over a poker game somewhere near Bijou Basin.)

By then, I'd reached Clay, who had rolled onto his back, a dazed expression on his face, his right hand pressed against the blood-pumping wound in the center of his chest. I shouted for someone to get a doctor, and saw some man go dashing toward the lobby. Clay attempted to sit up, but did not have the strength, and slumped back.

Hastily, I knelt beside him and removed my coat to form a pillow underneath his head, then wedged my handkerchief between his fingers and the wound. As I did, he looked at me as though I were a stranger. Finally, he blinked and, to my startlement, began to chuckle. "The one time I di . . ." I could not make out the rest. "What, Clay?" I asked distractedly, wondering if I should try to stop the bleeding in some other way.

He chuckled again. "The one day I did not reload," he repeated with effort. "Ben would laugh at that."

He swallowed, then began to make a choking noise, a trickle of blood issuing from the left-hand corner of his mouth. "Hang on," I said, pressing my hand to his shoulder. "The doctor will be here directly."

He shook his head with several hitching movements. "No sawbones can remove me from *this* tight," he said.

He stared up at the ceiling now, his breath a liquid sound that made me shiver. I did not know what to say, but could only keep directing worried (and increasingly angry) glances toward the lobby. "Where *is* he?" I muttered.

Clay made a ghastly, wheezing noise, then said, "My God." His fingers closed in, clutching at the already blood-soaked handkerchief. "I am going to die." Another strangling breath. "And I am only thirty-one years old."

Instant tears distorted my vision. *Thirty-one?*

Clay murmured something I could not hear. Automatically, I bent over and he repeated, in a labored whisper, "She was such a pretty girl."

"Who?" I asked; could not help but ask.

"Mary Jane," he answered. He could barely speak by then. Straightening up, I saw the grayness of death seeping into his face and knew that there were only moments left to him.

He made a sound which might have been a chuckle had it not emerged in such a hideously bubbling manner. His eyes seemed lit now with some kind of strange amusement. "I could have married her," he managed to say. "I could still be there." He stared into his fading thoughts. "Then I would never have . . ."

At which his stare went lifeless and he expired.

I gazed at him until the doctor came. Then the two of us lifted his body—how *frail* it was—and placed it on a nearby table. The doctor closed Clay's eyes and I crossed Clay's arms on his chest after buttoning his coat across the ugly wound. Now he looked almost at peace, his expression that of a sleeping boy.

Soon people began to enter the dining room. In a short while, everyone in Silver Gulch, it seemed, had heard about Clay's death and come running to view the remains. They shuffled past his impromptu bier in a double line, gazed at him and, ofttimes, murmured some remark about his life and death.

As I stood beside the table, looking at the gray, still features, I wondered what Clay had been about to say before the rancorous voice of Billy Howard had interrupted. He'd said that he had learned what fear is, "though not fear of . . ." What words had he been about to say? Though not fear of other men? Of danger? Of death?

Later on, the undertaker came and took Clay's body after I had guaranteed his payment. That done, I was requested, by the manager of the hotel, to examine Clay's room and see to the disposal of his meager goods. This I did and will return his possessions to his family in Indiana.

With one exception.

In a lower bureau drawer, I found a stack of Record Books bound together with heavy twine. They turned out to be a journal which Clay Halser kept from the latter part of the War to this very morning.

It is my conviction that these books deserve to be published. Not in their entirety, of course; if that were done, I estimate the book would run in excess of a thousand pages. Moreover, there are many entries which, while perhaps of interest to immediate family (who will, of course, receive the Record Books when I have finished partially transcribing them), contribute nothing to the main thrust of his account, which is the unfoldment of his life as a nationally recognized lawman and gunfighter.

Accordingly, I plan to eliminate those sections of the journal which chronicle that variety of events which any man might experience during twelve years' time. After all, as hair-raising as Clay's life was, he could not possibly exist on the razor edge of peril every day of his life. As proof of this, I will incorporate a random sampling of those entries which may be considered, from a "thrilling" standpoint, more mundane.

In this way—concentrating on the sequences of "action"— it is hoped that the general reader, who might otherwise ignore the narrative because of its unwieldy length, will more willingly expose his interest to the life of one whom another journalist has referred to as "The Prince of Pistoleers."

Toward this end, I will, additionally, attempt to make corrections in the spelling, grammar and, especially, punctuation of the journal, leaving, as an indication of this necessity, the opening entry. It goes without saying that subsequent entries need less attention to this aspect since Clay Halser learned, by various means, to read and write with more skill in his later years.

I hope the reader will concur that, while there might well be a certain charm in viewing the entries precisely as Clay Halser wrote them, the difficulty in following his style through virtually an entire book would make the reading far too difficult. It is for this reason that I have tried to simplify his phraseology without—I trust—sacrificing the basic flavor of his language.

Keep in mind, then, that if the chronology of this account is, now and then, sporadic (with occasional truncated entries), it is because I have used, as its main basis, Clay Halser's life as a man of violence. I hope, by doing this, that I will not unbalance the impression of his personality. While trying not to intrude unduly on the texture of the journal, I may occasionally break into it if I believe my observations may enable the reader to better understand the protagonist of what is probably the bloodiest sequence of events to ever take place on the American frontier.

I plan to do all this, not for personal encomiums, but because I hope that I may be the agency by which the public-at-large may come to know Clay Halser's singular story, perhaps to thrill at his exploits, perhaps to moralize but, hopefully, to profit by the reading for, through the page-by-page transition of this man from high-hearted exuberance to hopeless resignation, we may, perhaps, achieve some insight into a sad, albeit fascinating and exciting, phenomenon of our times.

Frank Leslie
April 19, 1876

If you enjoyed this book, subscribe now and get...

TWO FREE

A $7.00 VALUE–

If you would like to read more of the very best, most exciting, adventurous, action-packed Westerns being published today, you'll want to subscribe to True Value's Western Home Subscription Service.

Each month the editors of True Value will select the 6 very best Westerns from America's leading publishers for special readers like you. You'll be able to preview these new titles as soon as they are published, *FREE* for ten days with no obligation!

TWO FREE BOOKS

When you subscribe, we'll send you your first month's shipment of the newest and best 6 Westerns for you to preview. With your first shipment, two of these books will be yours as our introductory gift to you absolutely *FREE* (a $7.00 value), regardless of what you decide to do. If you like them, as much as we think you will, keep all six books but pay for just 4 at the low subscriber rate of just $2.75 each. If you decide to return them, keep 2 of the titles as our gift. No obligation.

Special Subscriber Savings

When you become a True Value subscriber you'll save money several ways. First, all regular monthly selections will be billed at the low subscriber price of just $2.75 each. That's at least a savings of $4.50 each month below the publishers price. Second, there is never any shipping, handling or other hidden charges—*Free home delivery*. What's more there is no minimum number of books you must buy, you may return any selection for full credit and you can cancel your subscription at any time. A TRUE VALUE!

A special offer for people who enjoy reading the best Westerns published today.

WESTERNS!

NO OBLIGATION

Mail the coupon below

To start your subscription and receive 2 FREE WESTERNS, fill out the coupon below and mail it today. We'll send your first shipment which includes 2 FREE BOOKS as soon as we receive it.

Mail To: **True Value Home Subscription Services, Inc.** P.O. Box 5235
    120 Brighton Road, Clifton, New Jersey 07015-5235

13214

YES! I want to start reviewing the very best Westerns being published today. Send me my first shipment of 6 Westerns for me to preview FREE for 10 days. If I decide to keep them, I'll pay for just 4 of the books at the low subscriber price of $2.75 each; a total $11.00 (a $21.00 value). Then each month I'll receive the 6 newest and best Westerns to preview Free for 10 days. If I'm not satisfied I may return them within 10 days and owe nothing. Otherwise I'll be billed at the special low subscriber rate of $2.75 each; a total of $16.50 (at least a $21.00 value) and save $4.50 off the publishers price. There are never any shipping, handling or other hidden charges. I understand I am under no obligation to purchase any number of books and I can cancel my subscription at any time, no questions asked. In any case the 2 FREE books are mine to keep.

Name _____

Street Address _____ Apt. No. _____

City _____ State _____ Zip Code _____

Telephone _____

Signature _____
(if under 18 parent or guardian must sign)

Terms and prices subject to change. Orders subject to acceptance by True Value Home Subscription Services, Inc.

JAKE LOGAN
TODAY'S HOTTEST ACTION WESTERN!

___SLOCUM BUSTS OUT (Giant Novel)	0-425-12270-0/$3.50
___A NOOSE FOR SLOCUM #141	0-425-12307-3/$2.95
___NEVADA GUNMEN #142	0-425-12354-5/$2.95
___THE HORSE THIEF WAR #143	0-425-12445-2/$2.95
___SLOCUM AND THE PLAINS RAMPAGE #144	0-425-12493-2/$2.95
___SLOCUM AND THE DEATH DEALER #145	0-425-12558-0/$2.95
___DESOLATION POINT #146	0-425-12615-3/$2.95
___SLOCUM AND THE APACHE RAIDERS #147	0-425-12659-5/$2.95
___SLOCUM'S FORTUNE #148	0-425-12737-0/$2.95
___SLOCUM AND THE DEADWOOD TREASURE #149	0-425-12843-1/$2.95
___SLOCUM AND THE TRAIL OF DEATH #150	0-425-12778-8/$3.50
___SLOCUM AND THE STAGECOACH BANDITS #151	0-425-12855-5/$3.50
___SLOCUM AND THE HANGING PARTY #152	0-425-12904-7/$3.50
___THE GRANDVILLE BANK HEIST #153	0-425-12971-3/$3.50
___SLOCUM'S STANDOFF #154	0-425-13037-1/$3.50
___SLOCUM AND THE DEATH COUNCIL #155	0-425-13081-9/$3.50
___SLOCUM AND THE TIMBER KING #156	0-425-13138-6/$3.50
___SLOCUM AND THE RAILROAD BARON #157	0-425-13187-4/$3.50
___SLOCUM AND THE RIVER CHASE #158	0-425-13214-5/$3.50
___TOMBSTONE GOLD #159 (April 1992)	0-425-13241-2/$3.50
___SLOCUM'S WAR (Giant Novel) (May 1992)	0-425-13273-0/$3.99
___SLOCUM AND THE SHARPSHOOTER #160 (June 1992)	0-425-13303-6/$3.50

For Visa, MasterCard and American Express orders ($10 minimum) call: 1-800-631-8571

Check book(s). Fill out coupon. Send to:
BERKLEY PUBLISHING GROUP
390 Murray Hill Pkwy., Dept. B
East Rutherford, NJ 07073

NAME _____
ADDRESS _____
CITY _____
STATE _____ ZIP _____

PLEASE ALLOW 6 WEEKS FOR DELIVERY.
PRICES ARE SUBJECT TO CHANGE
WITHOUT NOTICE.

POSTAGE AND HANDLING:
$1.50 for one book, 50¢ for each additional. Do not exceed $4.50.

BOOK TOTAL $_____
POSTAGE & HANDLING $_____
APPLICABLE SALES TAX $_____
(CA, NJ, NY, PA)
TOTAL AMOUNT DUE $_____
PAYABLE IN US FUNDS.
(No cash orders accepted.)

202d